"Why didn't you tell me? Why didn't you get word to me when it happened?" Landon asked.

"You had already joined the army by the time I realized I was going blind," Georgiana said. "And it was an accident."

"It was *that* accident, wasn't it?" He wasn't willing to let her shirk the issue or protect him from the blame. "The day you left the church so upset because of me."

She turned her head. She knew if she looked in his direction, he'd be able to tell she was withholding the rest of the story.

"I remember," he said, and took a small step toward her, unable to stay so far away.

"It was an accident, Landon. There wasn't anything anyone could have done to change it."

He couldn't believe she was trying to protect him from the truth. She should hate him, should totally blame him for her blindness, but she obviously didn't.

However, Landon w~~as~~ off the hook that ea~~sily~~

Books by Renee Andrews

Love Inspired

Her Valentine Family
Healing Autumn's Heart
Picture Perfect Family
Love Reunited

RENEE ANDREWS

spends a lot of time in the gym. No, she isn't working out. Her husband, a former all-American gymnast, co-owns ACE Cheer Company, an all-star cheerleading company. She is thankful the talented kids at the gym don't have a problem when she brings her laptop and writes while they sweat. When she isn't writing, she's typically traveling with her husband, bragging about their two sons or spoiling their bulldog.

Renee is a kidney donor and actively supports organ donation. She welcomes prayer requests and loves to hear from readers. Write to her at Renee@ReneeAndrews.com, visit her website at www.reneeandrews.com or check her out on Facebook or Twitter.

Love Reunited

Renee Andrews

Love Inspired

Recycling programs
for this product may
not exist in your area.

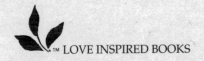™ LOVE INSPIRED BOOKS

ISBN-13: 978-0-373-81653-8

LOVE REUNITED

www.LoveInspiredBooks.com

Printed in U.S.A.

The Lord gives sight to the blind,
the Lord lifts up those who are bowed down,
the Lord loves the righteous.
—*Psalms* 146:8

This novel is dedicated to my oldest son, Rene Zeringue, and his beautiful new wife, Ariel Tingle Zeringue. May God bless each and every day of your life together.

ACKNOWLEDGMENT

Special thanks to Chief Warrant Officer 2 Johnny Matherne, Jr., for sharing his knowledge and insight for Landon Cutter.

As always, all mistakes are mine.

Prologue

"Don't marry him, Georgiana."

Georgiana Sanders stood alone in the center aisle of the Claremont Community Church and bit back the tremor of anxiety that rippled through her as she viewed the heart-shaped arch that would be covered in white roses in merely two days. Two days until she would be pronounced Georgiana Sanders Watson.

Cold feet. Every bride experienced the sensation, surely. She was no different. She swallowed hard. That had to be it.

Faint voices echoed through the empty church, the sounds of Brother Henry's wife and Georgiana's mother in the fellowship hall. But in spite of the fact that Brother Henry was in his office and the two women weren't far away, Georgiana felt very alone.

"Don't marry him, Georgie."

This time the voice was louder, stronger and extremely masculine. Definitely not imagined and undeniably familiar. She turned to see Landon Cutter, tall and muscled and beautiful, her neighbor and best friend since they were toddlers, standing merely a few feet away in the aisle.

Had he actually said the very thing that'd been haunting her heart?

"Landon?"

He stepped closer, and she caught a hint of the crisp woodsy scent of a guy that loved the outdoors. "I know you think he's changed," he said, "and I've prayed that he has, for you."

Georgiana blinked. Pete had changed. Everyone had seen the difference. He'd left his partying, bad-boy ways and had become a new person... for Georgiana. The whole town agreed. Everyone knew they'd get married. Everyone expected this wedding. "You don't believe he's changed?"

Landon's strong jaw flexed, as though he was trying to decide how much to say, but he was her best friend. He'd always told her the truth, and she didn't want him to stop now, not when it involved the most important decision of her life.

"Tell me, Landon."

"I don't know," he said, glancing at the front of the church and clenching that jaw again. His head subtly shook, and he continued, "Maybe he has, and maybe I shouldn't make this about Pete."

"Make what about Pete?" Her heart raced.

He moved even closer, looked at her with those amber eyes that she adored. Her best friend. Her confidant. The one who understood her better than anyone else, even better than the man she would marry in two days.

"I don't think you should marry him. Not just because I'm not a hundred percent certain that he's changed, but because…"

She looked into his eyes, focused on his words. "Because—what?"

"Because *I* want you. *I* love you. I believe I've loved you for years, but I never wanted to risk our friendship. And I could tell you had fallen for Pete. But…" He took a deep breath. "This was my last chance to tell you, and I decided I didn't want the chance to pass. I love you, and I wonder if you don't love me too." He eased his hands to her face, brushed calloused fingers along her jaw. "I want to be the one to kiss you in this church."

She knew what he was about to do. He moved closer, his mouth tenderly touching hers, hesitant at first, then exploring, and Georgiana found herself reveling in the feel of his arms circling around her, of the closeness they'd shared for the majority of their lives enveloping this embrace, this perfect kiss. For a moment, she simply lost herself in the amazing realization that she was kissing *Landon*.

A hint of voices in the distance reminded her of where they were and of the truth that her wedding was to take place in this church in merely two days.

The cake had been ordered. The church had been decorated. They'd had three wedding showers and had another scheduled for tonight. Pete's family had started arriving from out of town. Everyone in Claremont thought they should get married and had been anxiously waiting for this wedding.

She broke the kiss, tamped down on the emotion bristling through her very being. Landon. She had feelings for Landon. But she did love Pete. She did. And yet…

"I have to go." She turned from his embrace and ran from the church.

Landon watched her leave, strawberry-blond curls bouncing against her back as she retreated from his kiss…and ran closer to her wedding day. She was marrying Pete Watson, and Landon had now not only made a fool of himself in this church; he'd probably lost his best friend and the only girl he'd ever loved.

"God, please help me."

He took a deep breath, then heard the sound of a horn and the telltale sound of screeching tires that followed. Landon darted toward the door. "No!"

And then, as though the next sound was inevitable, it overtook the quiet with a deafening crunch of metal against metal in a loud *crash*.

Chapter One

Landon Cutter had only been home three times over the past eight years, but even though he'd stayed away from Claremont, Alabama, the majority of his lengthy tour of duty, he still hadn't been able to get Georgiana Sanders off his mind. The town reminded him of her. The farm reminded him of her. Ditto for the high school and the Claremont Community Church. Even the late August weather reminded him of Georgie. Because a decade ago, that'd been the time when the two of them spent so many hours talking about the new school year and all of their hopes and dreams while riding their horses through the Cutter fields and Lookout Mountain trails.

"What do you think, Sam? Reckon I can get used to this place again? Being back home?" he asked his best confidant and faithful companion, who didn't seem to mind the fact that Landon had left her with his brother John when he joined the army.

Sam's velvety lips brushed against his palm to scoop the molasses treat from his hand and then the stunning bay mare nudged his shirt pocket for more.

Landon grinned. Sam had always enjoyed her sweets, since the first day Landon's father brought her home from the Stockville horse auction. Landon was in eighth grade and had been pretty ticked that he'd been told he was getting a stallion and his dad bought the mare instead. While Landon was still brooding, Georgiana had ridden her own mare over from the next farm to see the new arrival. She'd instantly fallen in love with Samantha, who eagerly licked treats from her petite hand. After seeing Georgiana's approval, Landon decided that maybe his horse would do, but he was *not* calling her Samantha.

She'd been Sam ever since.

"Why don't we go ride the ridge for old times?" He glanced out the barn and across the expanse of land that separated the Cutter and Sanders farms.

Sam nickered as though she completely understood every word and every memory flooding his soul.

He gave her another treat. "Let's go, girl. It's been way too long, and I've got to get someone off my mind." He was finally back in Claremont, and Georgiana was still in Tampa, married to Pete Watson. It'd be good if he could remember that fact and would be even better if he could get his heart to do the same.

Ten minutes later, he and Sam were following the same route they'd taken every summer day back in high school and every fall evening after football practice. Georgiana never missed a ride, never missed a chance for the two of them to talk and grow closer. If Landon had a nickel for every time she told him that he was her best friend, he'd be rich. If he had a nickel for every time he wished she'd wanted more than friendship, he'd be filthy rich. And if Landon had one day to do over, it'd be that day he found her alone in the church and spilled his heart.

He shook his head, tried to stop thinking about the past and instead thought about the lyrics to a contemporary Christian song he'd heard on the radio today when John picked him up from the airport. *"You are more than the sum of your past mistakes."* Landon did his best not to show any emotions to the song, but John didn't miss a beat and wasted no time asking Landon if he was okay after the music ended.

Trademark answer. "I'm fine."

But he wasn't. He was still sick about the way

he'd left Claremont before, about the way he'd left Georgiana before. But leave it to his brother to give him plenty to keep his mind off the past.

"Listen, I should tell you that the economy has taken its toll on the farm," John said. "The demand and the price for beef has plummeted the past few years, and I haven't been able to figure out how to make everything work."

His brother's words shocked Landon. The farm was in trouble?

"I didn't want you to worry about it while you were serving," John continued, "and I thought I'd get the loans caught up before you got back. But—" he shrugged "—things only got worse."

"How bad is it?" Landon asked.

"Six months. That's how long we have. The bank has given us till the spring to turn a profit and bring the mortgage current."

John's words still echoed through Landon's mind as he and Sam made their way through the trails. They *couldn't* lose the farm. With their parents gone, the farm was all they had of the past, all they had of the Cutter property, land their family had owned for generations. And this property was amazing. Beautiful and pristine.

Sighing, he focused on enjoying Sam's smooth gait, the cool afternoon breeze against his face and the scents of hay, sweet feed, alfalfa and leather that blended around the farm, then the equally invigorating smells of cool crisp pine and damp earth as he made his way through the trails. The North Alabama surroundings were vastly different from the dry, dusty air and rancid odors from his time overseas.

But the tangible differences weren't the biggest contrast to his life overseas and his life at home. His disposition created the biggest difference of all. There he'd felt a continual sense of duty, but here he felt something totally opposite. *Freedom,* what he'd worked so hard to help maintain over the past eight years. In spite of the financial problems with the farm, he felt free now in the open fields, towering mountains and natural trails, and the beauty of it touched his heart. However, the splendor also reminded him of how he'd hoped to experience this countryside again one day, with Georgiana by his side.

After her wreck way back then, he'd vowed that he would never hurt her again.

He'd enlisted the next day.

Landon shook his head and attempted to shake those thoughts away. "The past is the past," he muttered. "I need to keep it there." But that wouldn't be easy now that he was back home, where memories filled his thoughts with every sight, every sound, every smell.

Sam seemed excited as she deftly maneuvered through the narrow trail, her hooves creating faint crushing sounds against the leaves and pine straw. "You like this as much as you used to, don't you, girl?" Landon guided her between towering purple rhododendrons and white mountain laurel. Georgiana had loved it when the mountain foliage bloomed. She'd said it was God's way of reminding you that He created these mountains.

Landon had told himself he would merely ride the Cutter acreage, take in the fields, check out the Charolais cattle and then maybe enjoy a little time by the pond. But deep down, he knew he wasn't sticking to the family land. Just like Sam, he realized exactly where they were headed, to the same place they always went before life got so complicated. No, Georgiana wasn't there any longer, and no, they hadn't even spoken since that awful night so many years ago, but he simply had to see the ridge where they had often sat and talked, where Landon often dreamed he'd kiss the girl he loved.

The flat rock that overlooked the Sanders property showcased the picturesque scene of Georgiana's family home. It looked exactly the same as it did back then, an almost exact replica of the Cutter farm, with a big two-story log home in the center surrounded by fields and ponds, cattle and horses, and a large Mennonite barn. The only difference, where the Cutter barn was red, the Sanders barn was forest green.

Landon searched the horses in the field for Fallon but didn't spot Georgiana's palomino. He wondered if Pete might have bought a horse farm in Tampa and taken Georgiana's favorite mare. That's what Landon would have done, if he and Georgiana had married and he'd taken her away from Claremont. Then again, if they'd married they would have stayed in Claremont, close to family and friends.

A movement by the green barn caught Landon's eye, and he watched as a striking horse sauntered into its paddock. The golden coat, stark white mane and equally white tail gleaming in the twilight gave Landon no doubt that this was Fallon. So Pete hadn't taken Georgiana's horse after all. Landon wasn't surprised Fallon was still at the farm though. Mrs. Sanders would never sell Georgiana's favorite mare.

He glanced toward the log cabin and thought he saw a shadow pass by one of the windows. Georgiana's mother lived there alone now, he guessed. Her father had passed away when Landon and Georgiana were seniors in high school, just three years after Landon's father had died. Landon had gone to the funeral, where Pete had stayed by Georgiana throughout the ceremony and held her while she cried. But that evening, when she wanted to ride the ridge and quietly reflect on her father's life, Landon was the one by her side. He'd understood what she was going through, having lost his own dad. Even if her father died of a heart attack and his had died in a farming accident, they'd both died way too young. And that night, when she'd sobbed until she fell into an exhausted sleep, Landon had been the one to hold her when she cried.

A few cows lifted their heads to glance toward Fallon as she neighed from her paddock, her long neck stretched as though trying to get the most enjoyment from the setting sun. Landon was so absorbed in watching Georgiana's horse that he nearly didn't see the second movement at the barn. But sunlight catching long strawberry-blond hair quickly drew his eye and held him captive.

She wore a green T-shirt, fitted jeans and boots. Her hair, even longer than in high school, was clipped back somehow and formed a red-gold waterfall of curls that fell nearly to her waist. She didn't readily move away from the barn, but stood nearby staring into the fields, her face tilted toward the sun so that Landon could see her clearly and had no doubt...

Georgiana.

Apparently sensing Landon's exhilaration, Sam

nickered happily, and Georgiana turned and looked directly toward the flat rock, directly toward Landon.

His breath caught in his throat, heart thundered in his chest. How many nights in the heat of turmoil in Afghanistan did he dream of seeing her one more time? And now that the dream was reality, he had no idea what to do. He lifted a hand and knuckled his Stetson. Then he waited, hoped, prayed.

But instead of returning the greeting, she turned away from the mountain and toward the house, where the front door had opened and a young girl scurried down the porch steps. She called something to Georgiana, but Landon couldn't make out her words. Even from his vantage on the ridge, he could see Georgiana smile, and then he clearly saw the girl, her hair the identical hue as her mother's but shorter and curlier. She looked around six or seven, Landon supposed, which went along with what he'd heard about Georgiana's pregnancy back when he'd still asked John about her in e-mails. After that e-mail announcing her pregnancy, Landon had stopped asking, and John hadn't volunteered.

So it was true; Georgiana had the little girl she'd always wanted. Landon suddenly wanted to know the child's name and whether she loved horses as much as Georgiana always had. Did she have that deep throaty laugh like Georgiana? Did she talk nonstop when she was excited like Georgiana? Was her nose sprinkled with copper freckles that spilled onto her cheeks like Georgiana's?

And did Pete Watson appreciate everything God had blessed him with the way he should? *Had* he changed back then, the way Georgiana thought? Landon had prayed that his quarterback would settle down, truly stop the wild partying ways and treat Georgiana the way she deserved.

The little girl said something else, caught up to her mother and took Georgiana's hand. Georgiana squatted down eye-level with her daughter, stroked her fingers down her little girl's curls and then pulled her close.

Landon's throat thickened. It wasn't right for him to watch them this way, and it certainly wasn't right for him to long for Georgiana this way.

God, help me understand why she isn't mine.

Then Georgiana slowly stood and Landon held his breath as, once again, she turned toward the mountain. Should he wave? Could she see him on the ridge? And now the little girl looked too.

Landon waited. If they acknowledged his presence, he'd simply have to ride down and say hello. With the way the sun was setting and the fact that he was at the edge of the tree line, he wouldn't think he'd be easily spotted. But if they had indeed seen him, then the neighborly thing to do would be to ride down. However, chances were that Georgiana and her daughter weren't the only ones visiting from Tampa. Pete would undoubtedly be at the Sanders home too. And Landon wasn't certain whether his old friend would find the gesture neighborly at all. Pete knew how much Landon had loved Georgiana. If anyone knew, it was Pete.

The little girl shielded her eyes from the brightness of the setting sun and scanned the mountain then she stopped and pointed toward Landon. "Hey!" she yelled, her voice loud enough now that Landon heard clearly.

He lifted a hand, started Sam toward the Sanders farm and prayed that God would give him the courage to get through whatever happened next.

Georgiana used to love watching the sun set against the backdrop of the mountains, the orange-gold sphere easing its way behind the trees and putting the farm in a majestic glow as it dipped. She took a few steps out of the barn into the open air, turned her head toward the direction where she knew the sun was setting and imagined seeing it again. The vision was beautiful; she knew that. And that should be enough. She shouldn't have to see it to know.

She merely had to remember.

But memories of sunsets brought back memories of Landon Cutter. How many sunsets had they viewed together growing up? And how many times had she felt a little hint that there might have been more between them than friendship? Why hadn't she acted on that? And why had he waited until that day in the church to tell her that he did feel something? And, more important than any other question, why hadn't she simply told him how she felt instead of running away?

She heard a horse nicker in the distance, and it didn't seem to come from the fields, so she tilted her head and listened again.

"Mom, don't you wanna come in and get ready to go to town?" Abi called, causing all of Georgiana's attention to turn toward the house, where the sound of her daughter's feet grew louder as she quickly progressed across the yard.

If Georgiana hadn't run away from Landon at the church back then, she wouldn't have her daughter. And even if that meant she was now blind, she wouldn't take anything for the extraordinary little girl that held her heart. "Hey, sweetie. I wanted to wait until the sun set. Then I'll come in and get ready."

Abi bounded into her mother, her arms wrapping around Georgiana's waist in a bear hug.

"Okay, I'll watch it with you," she said happily. "Then we'll go to town."

Georgiana smiled, squatted down to Abi's level. She ran her palm along her daughter's soft curls, the ones that were supposedly the exact same shade as Georgiana's. How she'd love to see her little girl's red hair, or her smile—Pete's wide dashing smile, she'd been told—or her eyes, which were apparently hazel like Georgiana's.

"It doesn't take too long to set, does it?" Abi asked. "'Cause I'm ready to go find you a new dress for my recital. It's in three weeks. That's what Mrs. Camp said."

The other children had been practicing for the recital all summer, while Abi had stayed with Pete. She would be the newest student with Mrs. Camp, but Georgiana's gung ho little girl didn't want to wait for the winter recital to show off her new skills. And she expected her mom to be at her first recital, naturally. Abi had taken lessons in Tampa, but they were given at a school that didn't do recitals for beginner students. Here, where Mrs. Camp gave all lessons in her home, a recital occurred for all levels every quarter. It was a pretty big deal for the kids.

Georgiana remembered how excited she'd always been to show her parents what she'd learned at each of her recitals. Mrs. Camp would make cookies and have punch for the kids, coffee and tea for the adults. And everyone dressed up for the event. Mrs. Camp had apparently described how the process worked to Abi, and now Georgiana's little angel had decided that all three of them, Abi, her grandma and her mother, needed new dresses for the big event. Abi and Eden had already purchased their outfits for the occasion, and tonight they planned to get one for Georgiana too.

"Three weeks is plenty of time to find a dress for me," Georgiana said. "We could wait till another night if you want." She had no desire to leave the farm, not tonight—or ever—but she had to for Abi, somehow.

"No, Mom, you promised we'd go tonight. And you said you'd let me pick it out. Remember? And we're going to get some candy at that candy store Grandma told us about too, remember?"

"I remember." The Sweet Stop. The old-fashioned candy shop had been Georgiana's favorite store on the square growing up. Well, that and the Tiny Tots Treasure Box, the local toy store. She did want to take her daughter there, but she wished that there wasn't such a drastic possibility of her running into half of Claremont when they went to the square. On a late summer night this cool, this comfortable, everyone would want to enjoy the beauty of town.

God, let the place be uncommonly deserted.

"So, does it take long for the sun to set?" Abi continued. "I'm really ready to go to town."

"No, it doesn't. In fact, it should be heading behind the trees now, if Fallon's timing is still spot-on." Resolved that there was no way she could get out of going to the square, Georgiana slid her hand into Abi's and stood. "Is that where the sun is, going behind the trees?"

"Yep, that's where it is," Abi said. "Well, almost. It sure does take its time, huh?"

"Yes," Georgiana said, gently squeezing Abi's hand, "it does." Then she heard the horse in the distance again. "Abi, do you hear…"

"Hey!" Abi yelled. "Mom, there's a guy on a horse up there. He's waving."

Georgiana's arm jerked as Abi apparently used her other hand to wave back. "A guy on a horse?"

"Yep, and I think he's coming to see us. Yep, yep, he is."

"What does he look like, Abi?" A guy on a horse? If Abi was waving in the direction that it seemed, then the guy was on the ridge, probably coming from the direction of the Cutter farm. Georgiana's mother had said John Cutter was running the farm now and that he'd been in charge ever since their mother died after Landon joined the army. And John was supposedly raising their younger brother, Casey. So this guy on the horse could be John or Casey. "Is he older, Abi? A man? Or is he a boy, you know, like a teenager?"

"He's a man," Abi said. "A cowboy, with a real cowboy hat and everything. And a pretty horse. Not as pretty as Fallon, but a pretty brown horse. A lot like Fallon though, except Fallon is gold and white, and this one is brown and black."

A pretty brown-and-black horse. "Sam?"

"What?" Abi asked.

"Nothing, honey. So the man is coming this way?" She knew he was. She could hear the horse's hooves clopping against the earth as the "cowboy" evidently came off the mountain and crossed the field. He moved slowly, judging from the sound of the horse's gait, and Georgiana used his slow arrival to gain her composure.

God, I asked You to help me not run into anyone I know tonight when I go to town. Did I need to ask that I not run into anyone before we go to town? Is this John? Or little Casey? Last time I saw Casey he'd been ten. He'd be eighteen now. Goodness, he's a man too, isn't he? And God, if it is either of them, please keep them from telling Landon that I'm blind.

Georgiana cleared her throat. There had been a few instances over the past few years where she was able to fool people into thinking she could see. Her eyes didn't look any different than normal according to her doctors. She simply had to concentrate on where to direct her attention or find a way to avoid eye contact. She could pull that off until John or Casey was gone, surely.

Stay with me, Lord.

"Hey!" Abi said again. "I like your horse."

"Thanks," the deep baritone answered. A familiar baritone that sent a ripple of awareness over Georgiana's entire body. "Her name's Sam."

"That's a funny name for a girl," Abi said, while Georgiana focused on keeping her balance. Her knees suddenly felt weak. Head started to swim. And if she really wanted to, she could totally throw up. Her stomach pitched enough, for sure.

"Yeah, well, it's short for Samantha," he said, a light chuckle in his words. The chuckle that used to make Georgiana laugh automatically in response. He didn't say anything for a second then said, "Hello, Georgiana." He paused. "Georgie."

Landon. Not John. Not Casey. But Landon. She couldn't speak, couldn't move. And hearing him call her by the nickname that'd been his alone sent a tremor down her spine.

"Mom?" Abi coaxed, and when Georgiana didn't respond, she yanked on Georgiana's hand for good measure. "Mom? You okay?"

Georgiana glanced in the direction of his voice.

"Hello, Landon." She could feel her cheeks heating, prayed they weren't as red as they felt. "I—I thought you were still overseas."

"Just got back today," he said. "Y'all home for a visit?"

One quality of her blindness, Georgiana had a precise sense of intonation, and she detected the additional question in Landon's words. Are you *and Pete* home for a visit?

"We're staying at Grandma's now," Abi enlightened. "I like the farm. Grandma lets me take riding lessons when the other kids have them. Do you have a farm too? Are you a real cowboy? How many more horses do you have? And do you just have horses, or do you have cows and chickens and stuff too, like Grandma does? Are all of your horses brown and black, or do you have other colors too, like we do? Hey, guess what? I'm six, but I'll be seven in September, after I go back to school."

There were many times that Georgiana loved her daughter's ability to fill the air with words. This was one of them.

Landon laughed. "Have mercy, you remind me of someone I knew when I was your age. She talked almost as fast as you do. What's your name?"

"My name's Abi, and you're talking about my

mom, aren't ya? Grandma says I'm just like she was when she was little. And Grandma says that she was a talker, like me."

"I'd guess that's true," he said. "What do you think, Georgie? Is she just like you?"

She made certain to look toward the sound of his voice and said in as clear a tone as she could muster, "Yes, she is."

"That isn't a bad thing." He waited a beat. "Not a bad thing at all."

"That's what Grandma says too," Abi said with a laugh.

"Abi, honey, you've got a phone call," Eden Sanders called. Georgiana pictured her mother walking out onto the porch, seeing Georgiana and Abi beside Landon Cutter and freezing in her tracks. But leave it to her mom; she must have recovered from the shock fairly quickly, because she hardly paused before adding, "It's your daddy, honey. You want to come talk to him inside, so you can hear better?"

And so Landon couldn't hear Abi's end of the conversation, no doubt.

"Sure!" Abi said, letting go of Georgiana's hand and starting to run away, but then her steps stalled, and she said, "Nice to meet you, Mr. Landon. You gonna bring your horse back to see us again?"

"Maybe so," he answered, and Georgiana wondered exactly how close Abi had been to the phone when she said Landon's name. Had Pete heard?

But before she could give that too much thought, she heard her mother's steps growing closer and smelled a hint of her floral perfume. "Mom, did you know Landon was home?"

"No, I didn't," her mother said. "It's wonderful to see you, Landon. Are you between deployments or home for good?"

"Home for good, Mrs. Sanders. And it's nice to see you too. Been a long time."

"Too long," she answered. "You living back at the farm?"

"Yeah, I'm planning to help run the place for a while. Still got some things to get worked out with John, but when it's all said and done, I'd like to stay there from now on."

"That's nice. It's good when land stays in the family. That's what my daddy always said. This was the land I grew up on, you know."

"Yes, ma'am, it is good to keep it in the family. That's our plan too."

"Well, I guess I'd better get back inside. We've promised Abi a trip to the square tonight to do a little shopping and go by the candy store. It really was good to see you, Landon." She paused, and Georgiana could almost see her mother smiling toward the boy—now man—that she'd always liked so much. "I hope you'll come visit often."

If Georgiana could glare at her mother, she would. There was no denying her tone was asking Landon—maybe even begging him—to spend time with her daughter. And she had no idea whether Landon had figured out the truth of her disability yet. If he had, it hadn't been indicated in his voice. But once he knew, he wouldn't want to spend time with Georgiana, not in the way her mother hoped. Or if he did, it'd only be because he felt sorry for her, and that wasn't what Georgiana needed at all.

She heard footsteps leaving and realized that her mother wasn't helping her get away from Landon. Eden could've easily said, *"Come on, Georgiana, let's go inside and get ready to head to town,"* but she didn't. Didn't she know that he'd figure out the truth if Georgiana merely stood here? "I should go inside too," she said. "It really was good talking to you, Landon."

She felt a movement to her left and instantly realized her mistake. When she'd been listening to her mother leave and wondering how to also head to the house, Landon and Sam had shifted to the left. But Georgiana had continued looking to the spot where they'd been, and she'd spoken to dead air.

The silence was worse than if he said anything,

and Georgiana didn't think she could stand hearing pity in Landon Cutter's voice, so she turned toward the house and walked away.

Chapter Two

John was waiting on Landon when he returned to the house and barely let him change clothes before ushering him to the truck. "I was hoping we could talk some about the farm when I got in from work, but I couldn't find you. We'll have to talk later, though, because we're meeting Casey at the square. You left your cell phone here so I couldn't reach you."

"My habit of carrying a cell phone kind of flew out the window over the last eight years," Landon said distractedly as he climbed in the cab and rubbed his forehead. What had happened to Georgiana in the time he'd been gone?

John rounded the front of the truck and got behind the wheel. "What's going on with you? You look like you've seen a ghost or something. Where'd you go with Sam, anyway?"

"To the Sanders farm. And she was there, John."

"Who? You mean Georgiana? She's home?"

"Yes, Georgie's home."

"I thought she was in Tampa with Pete. I didn't think they came home for visits at all." He cranked down the window on the old truck. "Anytime I asked Eden how Georgiana was doing and why we never saw her anymore, she said that Pete's job didn't leave a lot of time for traveling. I know Eden has gone down there occasionally over the years. She'd ask me to keep an eye on her farm while she was gone. But I don't think I've seen Georgiana back in Claremont since she and Pete got married. Odd that she's back on the same day you get back, huh?"

"Yeah, odd." Lots of things were odd about seeing Georgie today. Most of all what he'd determined right before he left her farm.

"Was Pete there too?"

"No, but he called their daughter while I was there. I guess he could've been calling from somewhere around here, but I got the impression he's still in Tampa. Their little girl's name is Abi, and she's the spitting image of Georgie when she was little."

"I'm sure I'll see her if they're staying in town a while." John paused, then asked, "So, how'd Georgiana look? Still the same? And how did you handle seeing her again?"

Too many questions, and each one could warrant an extensive answer. But only one thing mattered to Landon, and there was only one thing he wanted to tell his brother. He kept seeing Georgiana speaking to him, talking to him, but he'd known the entire time that something was off. Her eyes. They were still that stunning hazel he remembered, but the light that shone through them was gone. "She's blind, John. Georgiana's blind."

"What?" John stopped the truck at the end of the driveway and turned to face his brother. "What are you saying? You mean, like really blind? She can't see?"

"No, she can't see." And Landon suspected she hadn't been able to see in quite a while. Obviously she'd attempted to hide the truth from him, speaking to him as though everything was normal. But he'd sensed that something was off, and then at the end, when Sam had taken a couple of steps to the side and Georgie continued talking toward where they'd been, the truth hit Landon with the same force as that bullet in Afghanistan. Catching him unaware. Unprepared.

John shook his head and started the truck down the road leading to town. "How? Did she say what happened? When it happened? Do you think it's temporary? Is that why she's home, to let her mom help take care of her until she's better?"

Landon hadn't considered that. "I don't know."

"Well, I see Eden often, at church and around town. She's never mentioned anything about Georgiana losing her sight. Seems like she'd have said something."

"Unless Georgie asked her not to."

"Why would she do that?" John asked.

"Maybe she didn't want me to know," Landon pondered aloud. Georgie would have known that he would've wanted to help her if she was hurting. He would have done whatever he could to get home and be with his friend if she were in trouble. But she'd also have known that he was serving his country and wouldn't have wanted him to do anything differently because of her. And then there was the whole Pete factor. No way would Pete want some other guy coming home to check on his wife. "I can see her keeping that from me, especially while she knew I was still serving."

John grabbed his old baseball cap off the seat and put it on. "I can see that, I guess."

"Still can't believe it," Landon said. "She looks exactly the same. There doesn't seem to be anything wrong, except she can't see." His heart ached for Georgie. How long had she been this way? "She definitely didn't want me to know. I'm fairly certain she was trying to disguise the fact."

"How do you disguise it? Couldn't you tell looking at her? Or was she wearing sunglasses?"

"No sunglasses. And her eyes looked normal, but you know, like she wasn't really paying attention. Kind of like someone daydreaming."

"She didn't have a cane?"

Landon shook his head. "No, she didn't have anything like that."

John's mouth quirked to the side, brows dipped, and then he nodded. "Maybe she doesn't need one. I mean, think about it. When the power goes out at the farm at night, we can't see our hand in front of our face, but we still find our way around. Spatial memory, I think it's called. Or something like that."

"Yeah," Landon said. "That's probably it." But his thoughts weren't really focused on how Georgiana got around. He was more concerned with why she'd lost her sight to begin with. And he also wondered where Pete was while his blind wife and their daughter were at the farm.

John pulled into a parking spot behind one of the shops on the square. "Think you can stop thinking about it long enough to have dinner with our little brother?"

Landon nodded. "I'll try. Why are we meeting Casey at the square instead of having dinner at the farm?"

"Because he leaves for the University of Alabama next week, and he's trying to spend as much time as possible with Nadia Berry before he goes." John grinned. "He'll be home late tonight, so I thought it'd be nice for all of us to eat together. Nadia works at Carter Photography and is joining us for dinner." He paused. "I haven't told Casey about the troubles with the farm."

"Good. I don't want anything keeping him from going to college," Landon said.

John nodded. "And he'd stay here and try to help if he knew. All that kid has on his mind right now is spending as much time as possible with Nadia before he leaves. And, oddly enough, a pretty girl takes rank over his brother returning home from the army."

Landon smiled, thought of another pretty girl he'd seen a few hours ago. A beautiful blind girl. "I get it." He had another idea that might lend him a bit of information about what had happened to Georgiana. If any of their old friends were still in town, maybe she was still close to some of them. And maybe someone could enlighten him as to how she lost her sight. "You see any of the old gang while you're around town? I mean, did most of them stick around Claremont, or have they moved off?"

"Most have stuck around. Chad, Mitch, Daniel.

They all still live in Claremont. But I haven't seen anyone much over the past couple of years. Just the ones I see when I get to go to church," John said. "Too busy."

Landon realized that he hadn't acknowledged everything John had done over the past few years, taking care of Casey after their mother died and while Landon was still serving overseas. But he had a plan for letting John know how grateful he was, and he'd put that plan in motion soon. For now though, he simply said, "Hey, I appreciate everything you did for Casey, working yourself to death and saving for his college."

"I didn't touch his college money to help with the farm. There has to be another way." John glanced at Landon. "I thought you'd agree."

John had handled so much on his own.

"I do agree. Casey needs to go to school, and we *will* save the farm." Landon shook his head. "I should've come home after Mom died."

"We aren't going there again," John said. "All of that 'oldest child should've taken care of this or that' stuff. You came home during the roughest part. That was the important thing."

Their mother had never been the same after they lost their dad. He'd only been forty-one when he lost his arm in the hay baler and bled to death on one of the back fields. Their mother had become a widow overnight and had sunk into a depression equally as fast. But Landon hadn't realized just how bad she was, that she'd given up on her life and turned her focus to pills to help her forget the pain…until he got that call in Afghanistan and came home for the funeral. John assured him he was fine on his own to raise their little brother and take care of the farm and then Landon went back to serve the remainder of his tour of duty. But now he wondered if he should've requested more than the allotted emergency leave.

"You did the right thing, going back," John said, able to read Landon's thoughts as well as he had when they were kids. "You were serving our country and fighting for our freedom, and there isn't anywhere else you should've been." He punched Landon's arm. "And that's as mushy as you're gonna get from me, so let's leave it at that."

"Works for me," Landon said, and thought that John would probably feel a bit mushy tomorrow too, but he'd wait until he actually took care of his surprise before he let his brother in on the fact. That was one thing about being away from his family and friends for so long. Landon was a bit more sentimental for it, appreciated life more, he supposed, and appreciated his brother's hard work immensely. Until he returned home today, he had no idea John had been working three jobs to keep the farm afloat. John never said a word in his e-mails, and Casey never said much about anything but school and sports.

Nor had John told Landon how he'd saved enough money to pay for all of Casey's college education. Or how Casey's auto accident last year had been the result of alcohol. No, John took care of all of that and simply told Landon after the fact, along with the news that Casey had fallen for Nadia and consequently found God through his relationship with Brother Henry's granddaughter.

Thank You, Lord, for Nadia. And thank You, Lord, for John. Help me to never forget everything he's done over the past few years for our family. And Lord, if it be Your will, let us find a way to save our farm.

"Here we are," John said, leading Landon toward the back of Nelson's Variety Store. "Look familiar?"

"Smells familiar." Landon got a full whiff of the hamburgers from the five-and-dime. Then he heard an abundance of squawking geese and remembered how they always gathered around the three-tiered fountain that centered the square. "Sounds familiar too."

"Yeah, those noisy birds are kind of taking over for some reason. They had an article on it in the paper," John said. "I've only been down here twice this year when I was getting Casey's senior portraits set up, but I try to stay in touch with what's going on through the paper and the church bulletins."

Landon nodded, reminded again of how much John had done over the years he'd been gone. His brother wasn't trying to gain admiration, though. On the contrary, John was merely stating the facts about his life. John was like that, always spouting his thoughts in black and white, which is why it didn't surprise Landon when he didn't hold back his opinion about Landon's life either.

With one hand on the Nelson's door handle, John waited before entering the store.

"What's up?" Landon asked.

His brother looked back at him. "You never got over her, huh? After all these years?"

For someone who didn't want to get all mushy, John sure pushed the limit, and if Landon started talking about how much he hadn't gotten over *her,* they'd go well beyond mushy. He might be pushing thirty now, but not only had he never gotten over Georgie, in his heart he didn't know if any other female would ever do. He'd always compare them to the girl he loved, and no one measured up. Wasn't fair to do a girl that way. Wasn't fair to do himself that way either.

"We going to get one of those hamburgers I'm

smelling or not?" he asked, and his brother had the courtesy to nod and stop probing.

"Sure."

In no time at all they were seated at one of the red vinyl booths with Casey and Nadia. Landon had embraced his youngest brother in a hug that he was fairly certain would've embarrassed him years ago, but something had changed in Casey and he hugged Landon just as tightly and told him he loved him, while Nadia beamed at her boyfriend.

"He talks about you often," she told Landon. Then she smiled and added, "Thank you for serving our country."

Landon was drawn to the pretty Asian girl's sweet smile, her honest admiration for his service and the way she made Casey's face light up with unhidden love. "I enjoyed serving," he said, "but I'll admit I'm glad to be home."

She nodded, and the four of them chatted over burgers, mostly about Casey's plans for heading to the University of Alabama on Monday. Landon tried not to stare at his baby brother, but he couldn't help it. John had sent photos over the years, but there was something so different about seeing Casey in person. He was a carbon copy of Landon and John, almost eerily so, with light brown hair that was a little longer than Landon would've liked, but probably right in tune with what was "in" for teens nowadays, a broad-shouldered build that said he worked out regularly and loved sports as much as his older brothers, deep dimples creasing both cheeks and a smile that said he was happy with life and with his place in this world. Or at least with his place right now, sitting beside Nadia.

"Hey, if you aren't going to eat that, I will," Casey said, pointing to the rest of Landon's hamburger and fries.

Landon had been enjoying the conversation and seeing his family so much that he'd stopped eating. He grinned, pushed the plate forward. "Have at it."

Within minutes, Casey inhaled the rest of Landon's meal while Nadia chatted about how much she enjoyed her job at the photography studio.

"Carter Photography?" Landon asked, remembering Mia and Mandy Carter. Mia had been a year behind Landon in school and in the same grade as John. Mandy had been several years younger. And Landon recalled John's e-mail about the tragedy in their family last year. "Who owns it now that Mia passed away?"

"Mandy is running it now," John said. "I don't guess I ever told you, but she married Daniel Brantley, and they've adopted Mia and Jacob's son, Kaden."

"You don't say." Landon was amazed at how

much things had changed. Then again, he'd seen the ultimate change this afternoon in Georgie. He knew it was a long shot, but he had to find out if Casey knew more about her return home than John. "I rode over to the Sanders farm today. Georgiana was there."

Casey's dark brows lifted. "Wow, I'd nearly forgotten about her, it's been so long since I've seen anyone over there but Mrs. Sanders. Seems like forever since Georgiana used to come spend time at the farm with you guys, but I remember her. She had long red hair and rode her horse over about every day."

Landon should have realized that Casey wouldn't know anything about Georgiana's return. Casey had only been ten when she left Claremont. He probably remembered a pretty older girl who came out to the farm to visit, nothing more, nothing less.

"Ms. Mandy took her little girl's picture yesterday," Nadia said.

"Georgiana's little girl?" Landon hadn't expected to get any information from Nadia.

She nodded, shiny black hair bobbing with the action. "Yes, her name is Abi, isn't it?"

"It is. You said she was at the photography studio?"

"Mrs. Sanders brought her in to have her picture made for her piano recital. Mrs. Camp likes to make a program with all of the performers' pictures, you know. She did that when I took piano lessons from her too. Abi's a really pretty little girl, with all of those red curls and freckles, isn't she?"

Landon recalled how much she looked like Georgiana. "Yes, she is."

"She's been coming to church with Mrs. Sanders the past couple of weeks."

"Abi has?" Landon asked.

Nadia nodded. "I've seen them there on Sunday mornings."

"But not Georgiana?" Landon asked. Georgie had attended church every time the doors were open when she was growing up.

"No, I haven't met Abi's mother yet."

Landon was baffled. What *had* happened to Georgie while he'd been gone?

"You done?" John asked, tossing his napkin on the table. "We could go check out the square, not that all that much has changed since you've been gone."

"It'd still be nice to see everything again." And in the back of his mind, Landon wondered if he'd see Georgiana too. Her mother and daughter had mentioned shopping tonight at the square.

Casey snagged a fry from Nadia's plate, popped it in his mouth and swallowed. "Sounds good to me," he said. "Okay for you?" he asked Nadia, who smiled and nodded.

They paid for their meal and then headed out to the town square. Landon studied everything as they started down the sidewalk. Night had settled in, so the tiny lights bordering each building's eaves cast the streets in a yellow tint. Children laughed around the splashing fountain, and several elderly couples sat on park benches tossing bread to the noisy geese. A family exited the Sweet Stop as Landon passed the doorway and a gust of sugary air hit him full force. He remembered Abi saying that she was going to the candy store and glanced in to see if Georgie was inside.

She wasn't.

"Casey and I went there earlier for some of the divinity. And they were making peanut brittle," Nadia said.

"I told Nadia we'd go back later and get that for dessert," Casey said, grinning. "Figured the divinity was an appetizer to our dinner."

"And since you ate your dinner and a bit of everyone else's," John said, "you definitely will need dessert."

"Yep, I will," Casey agreed, laughing.

Landon loved this, spending time with family. He'd missed it more than he realized. And he wondered what kind of family life Georgiana had now.

Her father had passed away over a decade ago. Her mother had primarily been in Claremont, visiting Tampa occasionally, but not seeing her daughter a whole lot from what John had said. And Georgiana had been in Tampa with Pete and Abi...blind.

What had she been limited to because of her loss of sight? Had Pete helped her adjust to her blindness? Had he been the type of loving, supportive husband he should have been? Landon recalled the Pete he knew in high school, always wanting the best and not wanting anything that was less than perfect. He'd always said Georgiana Sanders was "absolutely perfect." Landon had thought so too, but now he wondered if Pete still saw her in that light.

"There's Mr. Brantley and his friends," Nadia said, indicating a group of guys standing on the sidewalk outside of Carter Photography. She waved, and Chad Martin tossed up his hand with a smile, then his brows lifted, his smile broadened and he yelled, "Landon! Had no idea you were home, buddy. Is this it? You home for good?"

"Home for good." Landon closed the distance between them and gladly accepted several hugs and pats on the back from his old friends.

"Man, it's been a long time," Daniel said.

"Too long," Landon agreed.

They visited, and he couldn't help but notice

that he felt a little lost in local happenings and with life in general. He knew that often happened to guys that were in the service, but he'd never really thought about the possibilities of what might happen in eight years. Many of his friends had not only married, but also started having kids. Georgiana had as well, and she'd lost her sight. The pain and shock of *that* just wouldn't go away.

The group caught up on everything that had happened over the past few years, but Landon's mind hovered on Georgie. He tried to maintain a polite interest in the conversation but also kept a keen eye tuned around the square for the sight of that gorgeous redhead.

Within minutes, he saw the striking red hair, even if on a smaller beauty.

"Hey, Miss Mandy!" Abi yelled. Her curly strawberry pigtails bounced wildly against her shoulders as she sprinted toward the group and directed her question to Mandy Brantley. "Are my pictures ready yet?"

"Abi, it's great to see you again." Mandy touched one of the little girl's pigtails. "You just had your pictures made yesterday. Remember how I said it'd take a few days?"

"Yes, I remember, but I asked Grandma if I could come check, and she said yes. And I wanted to ask you about helping us tonight anyway. 'Cause we brought Mommy tonight for the first time for her to come to this town, and she needs some new shoes to go with the new dress we got her to wear to my piano recital, but Grandma doesn't know a whole bunch about cute shoes. And I told her how you had on cute shoes when you took my pictures. And you have cute shoes now too." She pointed to Mandy's colorful sandals.

"Thank you," Mandy said.

"So do you want to help us find Mommy some cute shoes while we're in town? We've been looking, but I can't decide. And neither can Grandma." Then, as though she just noticed the other people standing around with Mandy, she explained, "Grandma and I help Mommy pick stuff out so she can have the right colors and match it and all. Mommy says that's my important job, helping her pick the colors out. I know my colors, but I don't know kinds of shoes that good yet." She scanned the faces in the group, then stopped, hazel eyes popping when she got to Landon. "Hey, Mr. Landon! I didn't know you were coming to town too. Did you ride your horse?"

The whole group laughed, while Landon grinned. "Not tonight, Abi." He glanced behind her to find Georgiana and Eden, but a group of brawny teens wearing Claremont football jerseys hid his view. "So where are your Grandma and Mommy now?"

The football team moved toward and then past the group, and sure enough, Eden and Georgiana were right behind them.

"There they are!" Abi said, grinning and pointing.

Georgiana, now wearing a yellow floral sundress, green sweater and sandals, looked even prettier than she did back in high school. Her hair was no longer pulled up like it had been earlier, and it toppled in beautiful long swirls to reach her waist. He wanted to see her eyes, but she wore sunglasses in spite of the fact that it'd been dark for at least an hour.

"Hey, Mommy, I asked Miss Mandy if she'll help us find cute shoes to go with the red dress." She looked back to Mandy. "Are you gonna help us?"

Mandy laughed. "I'd love to."

She talked about Abi's photo shoot, but Landon barely heard their conversation. He was too busy examining Georgiana's face and disposition. Her fingers were wrapped snugly around her mother's forearm, he assumed to let Eden subtly lead her through the square. But then he noticed the tension in her forehead and the way her mouth seemed drawn and tight. And he noticed Eden did all of the talking, with Georgiana attempting to slide her mouth into a smile when appropriate. She looked anything but comfortable. In fact, Landon would say she looked miserable.

Then he realized Eden was helping her out by working the names of those present into her conversation. She didn't announce the fact that Georgiana was blind, but subtly told her daughter the members of the group.

"It's so good to see all of you together again," Eden said. "Seems like forever ago since all of you hung around in high school. Daniel, Mandy, Mitch, Chad…and Landon."

Landon didn't miss the fact that Georgiana's hand squeezed her mother's forearm when Eden said his name. Why was she uncomfortable around him? And why had she tried to hide her blindness from him earlier today?

"So Mandy, would you want to come with us to shop for shoes?" Eden asked.

"Yes, would you?" Abi coaxed. "Please."

"I'd sure appreciate the help," Georgiana said softly, and Landon noticed that she turned toward Mandy when she spoke. He also noticed that the group exchanged glances, indicating that they realized Georgiana couldn't see. Mandy obviously already knew, and it appeared Daniel did too, but Chad's and Mitch's faces didn't disguise their shock, even if they managed to keep their smiles in place for Eden and Abi.

"Mandy's always in the mood for shopping," Daniel said.

"That's right," Mandy agreed, "and I'd love to go now." She kissed Daniel, told him she'd be back in a little while, then asked, "So, do y'all have the dress with you?"

"Yep, it's in that bag," Abi said, pointing to a paper *Consigning Women* sack hanging from Eden's arm.

"Then I guess we're ready to go," Mandy said.

"Nice running into all of you," Georgiana added, then turned and walked away with her mother, Abi and Mandy.

A decade ago, Landon would have simply let her leave and then wondered why she seemed particularly uncomfortable around him or why she'd tried to hide her blindness from him this afternoon. But that was a decade ago. He'd lived a lot and learned a lot in the years between, and he wasn't about to merely sit and wonder this time.

"Georgiana," he called, and took the few steps to catch up to the group of females.

She paused, turned and waited.

Landon found himself swallowing through the automatic response to being face-to-face with her again. She'd always taken his breath away, and now he found it nearly hard to speak. But he *would* speak. And he *would* find out what had happened to her during the years they'd been apart.

"Yes?" she asked, a slight tremor in the single syllable.

"I'd like to come see you tomorrow at the farm, catch up on everything that's happened to us since high school, if that's okay."

Eden and Mandy locked glances and gave each other soft smiles that made Landon wonder what they knew that he didn't.

"Would that be okay?" he asked.

"I do riding lessons tomorrow," Abi said. "Maybe you could come watch me."

"I'd like that a lot," he said to the pretty little girl, then looked up at her striking mother. "Is that okay with you, Georgiana?"

The slightest hint of panic slipped over her features, but she masked it quickly. She did not want to talk to Landon; he was sure of that. But he was equally certain that he wasn't going to take no for an answer.

He took a step closer, leaned toward her ear and hoped the sounds of the geese squawking and people talking would drown out his whispered words. "Please, for old times. Let me come see you tomorrow. Spend some time with me, Georgie." He said a quick, silent prayer, then added, "Say yes."

Her slender throat pulsed as she swallowed. "Okay."

Chapter Three

Every morning since she'd moved back to the farm, Georgiana woke bright and early, then made her way out to the barn to spend time talking to Fallon and to God. Today was no different, except the need for quiet time was even more intense after last night's trip to the square.

Even though she hadn't lived here in years, it hadn't taken Georgiana long at all to remember everything, and consequently, she could easily make her way to the barn without need of her white cane. This was familiar. This was home.

As always, Fallon awaited her arrival, nickering softly when Georgiana neared her stall.

God, be with me today. You know how much I need your help. Keep me strong, Lord.

She'd actually enjoyed the majority of her time at the square last night, shopping with her mother,

Abi and Mandy. For a while there, she felt normal again.

Georgiana let the comfort of the barn envelop her as she tenderly stroked the smooth lines of Fallon's cheek and jaw. Fallon loved to be touched like this; that hadn't changed over the years, and Georgiana enjoyed the smoothness of her pelt against her palm. Being with Fallon reminded her of the past, the good memories rather than the bad, and she relished these mornings with her gentle friend.

Soft footsteps approached and the crisp scent of coffee mixed with the usual scents of hay, leather and horse filling the barn.

"Georgiana, it's me," her mother said softly.

She smiled. "I know, Mom."

"Thought you might want some coffee," she said, and eased the mug handle into Georgiana's palm.

"Thanks." Georgiana sipped the coffee, exactly the way she liked it, two spoons of sugar and a dollop of French vanilla cream. "Delicious."

"Mmm-hmm."

Georgiana felt her mother's arm reach past her to stroke Fallon. Fallon's warmth shifted too, eager to accept a bit of loving from both women.

"Where's Abi?"

"She wanted to eat her oatmeal and drink her

coffee milk at the hearth while she watches *Little Bear*."

"Right," Georgiana said, knowing her daughter's morning routine. The "coffee milk" portion had been added after they came to the farm. When Georgiana had been Abi's age, that'd been her morning treat as well, a mug of mostly milk and a little bit of coffee and sugar that made her feel like a big girl. She remembered the special sensation associated with getting that mug from her mom each morning and was glad her daughter could experience the same thing.

"*Dora* comes on right after *Little Bear,* and she'll want to watch that too," Eden said.

Georgiana knew this, of course, but she also knew why her mother reminded her, so she would realize that they had a full hour to themselves to talk. She swallowed another sip of hot coffee, let the richness of it warm her stomach and calm her fears of asking her mother's opinion. "Mom?"

"Yes?"

"I'm…I'm nervous about Landon coming over. Being around people I knew before, being around *him*—" she struggled for the right words "—it makes me—uncomfortable."

She heard her mother take another sip of coffee, a nearly silent sound but one Georgiana easily recognized. Eden was undoubtedly taking a moment to think, to make sure she said exactly the right thing, the way she always did. Then she gently pushed Georgiana's hair back from her shoulder and said, "Life would be rather boring if everything were always comfortable."

Georgiana's mouth quirked to the side. "Well, it certainly isn't comfortable now, is it?"

"No, honey, it isn't." Eden continued running her palm down Georgiana's hair in much the same way she did when Georgiana had been Abi's age. She wanted to soothe Georgiana's fears, put her at ease. But Georgiana wasn't sure that was possible.

"Mom, I probably shouldn't have told you what happened in the church that day. Nothing will change the fact that I ran away and had the wreck." She touched Fallon again. "And I'm sure Landon doesn't think I told anyone. He probably wouldn't have wanted me to tell anyone."

"Oh, sweetie, you know that isn't true. Landon loved you, and he came to the church to tell you. The only reason he didn't tell people himself is because you chose to still marry Pete. Even though your heart was thinking about someone else."

"Mom, I loved Pete. I did."

"Honey, I believe you. But there are different kinds of love. There's the kind of love that's, well, borderline infatuation. A little stronger than that, but still primarily fueled by the physical attraction you have for one another. And then there's the kind of love that lasts, the kind of love that can endure the toughest of storms. Physical attraction as well, of course, but deeper. Much deeper." She paused, then added, "Pete couldn't handle the storms, Georgiana. That isn't your fault, it's his."

"I couldn't be the kind of wife he wanted anymore." Georgiana's heart ached with the admission. "He's a partner in his firm. He has to make a statement to their clients and to the public in general. How was I supposed to blend with those country-club folks when I couldn't see? I had no idea what they were wearing, no idea where they were going. Plus I'd just had Abi and wanted to be with my baby."

"Honey, you don't need to explain to me. If that boy would have been a real husband, he'd have built you up at your lowest point instead of kicking you down. And don't you go defending him. I'll always care about him because he's Abi's daddy, but I don't think a thing of him for the way he treated *my* little girl."

"Mom, please. What guy would have stayed?" Eden didn't miss a beat. "I can think of one."

"You don't know that. And I wouldn't want anyone to stay with me out of pity."

"Georgiana, Pete has brainwashed you into thinking no one would want you now. I saw the way Landon looked at you last night, and there wasn't an ounce of pity to it. Longing maybe, but not pity."

A tiny trickle of hope worked its way into Georgiana's heart, but then just as quickly, she heard Pete's words.

"Good Lord, Georgiana. Look at you. Your hair looks like a troll doll and your clothes look like something from thrift-store central. I'm taking you to mingle with my colleagues. I can't take a wife that looks like that!" The sounds of slamming doors and several derogatory names Georgiana didn't want to remember, then *"Just forget it. I don't want you there anyway. Charity, you can go home. We won't need a babysitter tonight."* Then, to Georgiana, *"You can still handle taking care of our daughter, can't you?"* Another slamming door. And another miserable night by herself with Abi as her only comfort.

"Mom, Landon wouldn't want me now."

"I'm not going to listen to that kind of talk. A moment ago, you were starting to believe what I was saying. *That's* what you need to concentrate on, not everything that you heard from Pete. I mean that."

"I don't even know if Landon has someone in his life now. That is a possibility, you know. He could have married, had children…"

"Nope, and nope. He never married and didn't have kids. You forget I see John at church and he watches the place for me anytime I'm gone."

"You did *not* ask him if Landon had married."

"Dear, Claremont is a small town. I ask if everyone has married. And who has had kids. And who has passed on. Actually, half the time you don't even have to ask. It's right there every Sunday in the church bulletin."

"Nothing like gossip started in a church handout."

"It isn't gossip, dear. It's the announcements," Eden said, and Georgiana couldn't hold back her laugh.

"I love you, Mom."

"I know. I love you too." Eden gave her a tender hug. "Now remember that you are a fine catch, and I'm betting that there's a guy coming to see you today who knows that better than most."

"But Mom, you've forgotten the other problem with Landon and me talking again."

"What's that?"

"He still doesn't know what caused my blindness."

"So he'll ask, and you'll tell him," Eden said, as though that were all there was to it. But surely she knew it wasn't that easy.

"And then he'll blame himself."

"Honey, God has his reasons for everything that happens in life. And He had a reason for what happened on that day. *That's* what you'll have to tell Landon."

"Then pray that he doesn't blame himself? And pray just as hard that he doesn't blame me for not telling him?"

"He told you he loved you," her mother reminded. "Do you honestly think those feelings are gone?"

"Until yesterday we hadn't seen or spoken to each other in eight years. That's hardly what people do if they love each other." She finished her coffee, placed the empty mug on the top of the rail.

"He left because you chose Pete."

"And it's like you said, everything happens for a reason."

Her mother was silent for a moment, then whispered. "Georgiana?"

"Yes?"

"I think you're right. And if everything does happen for a reason, then I have to believe that Landon's return to Claremont right after you came home happened for a reason."

Georgiana wasn't expecting that. "Things change in eight years. *People* change in eight years."

"I saw it in his eyes last night, Georgiana. He

still cares about you. To what extent, I don't know, but he definitely still cares."

Georgiana wished she could've seen Landon's eyes, and she decided to ask the question she was dying to have answered. "Mom, about Landon."

"What about him?"

"What does he look like now? I mean, has he changed since high school, or does he still look the same?" She'd wondered ever since she heard that rich baritone yesterday afternoon, because in her mind she pictured the same gorgeous boy she'd known way back then. But time might have changed his appearance, and though it wouldn't change the way she felt about him, she was more curious than she cared to admit.

"Oh, he still looks the same as he did back then," her mother said.

"Does he?"

"Well, I mean, for the most part," Eden continued, and Georgiana could hear the smile in her tone. "He's broader, more muscled up, I guess you'd say."

"*More* muscled up?" That would be hard to accomplish, since he was at peak shape back in high school, the best running back Claremont ever had as far as she knew. Wide shoulders, lean waist and powerful thighs that he used skillfully whenever he needed another few yards to make a first down.

Or a touchdown. Landon had made his share of touchdowns during his career at Claremont High. Two more than Pete. Georgiana knew because Pete often complained about the fact and spouted the three plays where he could have scored if his line had only done their job, which would have put him over Landon's record.

"His hair is short too, army style," her mother continued. "That's the biggest difference, I guess, and he looks more like a man now, not a boy."

Georgiana nodded, wishing she could have seen the man her mother described. She'd never seen Landon with short hair. He'd always kept it long and wavy. Having his hair away from his face probably drew more attention to the chiseled jaw and the gold in his eyes. Landon was the only person she'd ever seen with eyes that were truly amber, like honey in sunshine.

"Same deep dimples," her mother said, still describing the guy that was slowly but surely controlling Georgiana's every thought. "They should outlaw those Cutter dimples. All three of them have those dimples, and even women as old as me notice. Landon, John and even that young Casey."

That made Georgiana laugh. "So you're saying Landon's still a decent body double for Matthew McConaughey?"

"I'd forgotten how you used to say that about

him," her mother said with a laugh, "but yes, he looks like him."

Georgiana nodded, thought about the gorgeous guy who'd been her best friend.

The barn grew quiet, with both of them evidently reflecting on how things could have been so different.

"Georgiana," her mother finally said.

"Yes?"

"You should try again."

She knew exactly what her mother was talking about, but still asked, "Try what?"

"Giving someone the chance to be there for you, to build you up instead of bring you down."

"I did, Mom. Pete and I tried marriage counseling."

"*You* tried marriage counseling."

"He came off and on," Georgiana said, then couldn't stop herself from adding, "It was hard for him to deal with it all."

"It was harder for you."

Georgiana couldn't argue with that. It *was* harder for her, no doubt. She was the one whose world had been upended, first with the move to Tampa and then with the loss of her sight and then finally with the abandonment of her husband. A triple whammy for sure.

"Honey, I know this hurts, but it needs to be

said. Pete left that marriage *before* you ever went to that counselor. The minute you lost your sight, I'd say. There wasn't anything left to save. I know that you feel like you don't have anything to offer to another person, but you do. And it's time for you to trust again, to trust someone not to break your heart."

There was no point in being anything but honest. "I don't think I can."

"I've prayed for you to learn to trust again. And I honestly think God answered my prayers with Landon's return home."

"Mom," Georgiana started, then decided to go ahead and tell her mother one part of the story she didn't know. "When he came to see me that night at the hospital, I told him not to come back, that I didn't want him in my life."

Her mother cleared her throat. "Well, now, it looks like he didn't listen."

"What do you mean?" Georgiana asked, then she heard what her mother must have already seen. A horse's steady gallop in the distance growing louder by the second. "I'm not even dressed to see anyone yet. I can't see him now. I thought he said something about seeing Abi at her riding lessons. Surely he knows that'd be later in the day." When Eden offered no response, Georgiana prompted, "Mom?"

"I'm going to head inside and check on Abi," she said, then added in a whisper, "He's the answer to my prayer, Georgiana. Let him help you."

"Wait," Georgiana pleaded, but her mother's footsteps steadily left the barn.

God, please, stay with me now. Help me, Lord. Keep me strong.

She reached out for Fallon, but the horse had obviously moved to the paddock, probably because she heard the other horse approaching. "Fallon? Come here, girl." She clicked her tongue against the roof of her mouth and hoped her horse cooperated. She didn't want to simply stand here and wait for Landon to enter the barn. She needed to be busy, needed to be doing something. "Fallon?"

But Fallon didn't answer, and all Georgiana heard was the other horse's steps easing to a stop. And then a bit of rustling as Landon obviously climbed off and tied Sam up. Slow and steady footsteps cautiously approached her in the barn. And Georgiana could do nothing but wait for the inevitable, being completely and totally alone with Landon.

Chapter Four

During Landon's time of service, he'd faced suicide bombers, roadside bombs and rockets hitting nearby. Throughout each and every harrowing situation, he'd controlled his fear. But right now, in an Alabama barn with Georgiana, he trembled.

Her hair toppled long and wild and free down her back, a mass of golden strawberry curls. She wore a pale blue T-shirt, gray plaid pajama pants, a charcoal fleece jacket and pink work boots. She faced him now but didn't see him, and that realization pierced his heart.

He swallowed thickly, determined to control his voice and hide the emotion wreaking havoc over his soul. "Georgie, we need to talk."

She blinked, moistened her mouth, then turned back toward the stall where Fallon had reentered and moved back to her owner. Georgiana's hand reached for the mare, and Fallon positioned her silky white mane against her palm. "I didn't think you would come this early," she said, and he noticed not only the tremor in her voice but also the shudder in her hand as she stroked Fallon's mane.

"I remembered how you always woke up early to see Fallon, and since I was up too, I rode over." He decided it best to keep his distance, because she was obviously uncomfortable with his arrival and because he didn't know if he could control himself to merely touch her without embracing her, without holding her the way he'd dreamed of holding her each and every night in the heat of battle. He'd thought he would never have that chance, because she was Pete's, but he suspected that was no longer the case. What had Pete done to ruin their marriage?

"You used to hate getting up early in high school," she said.

"That's because I wasn't a fan of having so much to do around the farm before I went to the morning football workouts. For most of the team, that was their first work of the day. I'd already been sweating hard for a couple of hours by the time I got to the field house." He shrugged. "That came in handy when I went to basic training though, so I shouldn't have complained." He stopped a few feet away from Georgiana. Fallon stepped toward him and sniffed his sleeve. "And I'm still adjusting to the time difference too, so my sleep is sporadic."

"What *is* the time difference?"

"We're nine and a half hours behind Kabul," he said. "Kind of throws off your sleep schedule."

"I bet it does." She continued stroking Fallon. "How was it over there? I mean, in general, what's it like? You hear things on the news, but I've never talked to anyone who has actually been there."

Landon hated this, making small talk when he wanted to delve into what they both were thinking, but he also hated the fact that she was apparently scared about this conversation. He hoped and prayed it was only the conversation and not him.

"Kabul. That's in Afghanistan?" she continued.

"Yeah. I was there a while, as well as a few other areas over the years. I spent some time in Kuwait. Some in Iraq. Mostly Afghanistan though."

"There've been a lot of injuries there," she said, then added, "a lot of deaths."

Landon nodded. He'd lost three of his best friends. Their names and death dates were now tattooed on the inside of his left wrist, but Georgie couldn't see that. She'd never see that. Then he realized she also couldn't see him nod and said, "Yes, there have been a lot of deaths. Way too many."

"Were you ever…" she started, then squinted as she reached again for Fallon. "Did anything happen to you over there? Were you ever hurt?"

He'd never lied to her before. He wouldn't start now. "Just once."

Her hand stopped stroking Fallon's mane, and she pivoted a little, providing Landon with a full display of her beauty, red-gold hair framing a heart-shaped face and showcasing an adorable sprinkling of faint copper freckles on her nose and cheeks…and those exquisite hazel eyes. He studied the full mouth that he'd kissed only once and the cheekbones that made her face automatically give the impression that she was about to smile, even if she wasn't.

Landon wondered how long it'd been since she released that ample smile he'd always loved. Or the laugh that echoed from her very soul. Even though she looked as though she *could* smile, she also had a tone that said she wouldn't, that maybe she couldn't. Her face portrayed a distance, an invisible wall, and Landon didn't think it was entirely because of her blindness.

"You were hurt?" she asked.

He'd been so absorbed in looking at her that he nearly lost track of the conversation. He cleared his throat. "It wasn't bad."

"*What* wasn't bad? What happened?"

"A clean hit to the shoulder. Went straight through."

Her mouth opened in a small O. "You were *shot?*"

"Like I said, it wasn't bad." Nothing at all compared to some of the other injuries he'd seen. Or the fatalities. His mind catapulted to that day when he had to identify the body of one of his friends. The image haunted him often at night, as did the sound of Calvin's parents when Landon called to offer his condolences. Yes, Landon had seen plenty during the past few years, but he wouldn't get into that now. That wasn't what he was here to talk about and certainly wasn't what she needed to hear.

"I'm so sorry that happened," she said, her voice strangled with the words. "I can't believe you were shot and no one told me."

Landon had an answer for that. "I'm pretty sure that's because no one knew."

"You didn't tell anyone? Not your family or your friends or anyone? What about John?"

"No, no one."

Her sightless eyes still held so much compassion that Landon's heart squeezed hard in his chest. "Why not?"

Georgiana's concern touched him in more ways than she could describe. He'd never told John because his brother had enough on his plate raising Casey. Plus the wound wasn't life-threatening. He didn't tell Casey, of course, because he was just a kid. And all of Landon's buddies in the unit already knew and merely thought of it as part of the job.

Landon hadn't had anyone who actually sympathized with him over the bullet that rocked not only his body but also his soul. He'd felt so defeated at that point. It was only six months after he'd lost his mother and for the briefest moment, he'd wondered if he'd let his guard down on purpose, if he'd wanted to get shot so he could see his parents again. And there hadn't been a single person that he could admit that to at the time.

What he would have given to have heard even one person sound as though they really cared, ask about him in the same tone he now heard from Georgiana. He swallowed through the flood of emotions her words created and answered, "There wasn't any reason to worry anyone. It wasn't all that bad."

She turned her head away. "No one should have to go through something that horrible alone."

Landon realized that she might very well be talking about more than his bullet. She might be talking about what *she* went through alone. "Georgie, why didn't you tell me about your blindness? Why didn't you get word to me when it happened?"

"You had already left the country by the time I realized what was happening."

"What *did* happen?" he asked. "What caused it?"

She kept her head facing Fallon, probably because she knew if she looked in his direction he'd see how much she hurt. She shrugged. "Three months after we were married, right after I found out I was pregnant with Abi, my vision started getting blurry. It was a gradual thing, but the doctors couldn't correct the problem, and eventually, I lost my sight completely."

"They don't know what caused it?" he asked.

Another shrug of her petite shoulders, then she whispered, "They couldn't tell for sure."

"I hate it that you went through all of that," he said, desperately wanting to comfort her and no longer able to keep his distance. He moved even closer, close enough to smell a hint of sweet apple shampoo enveloping the only woman he'd ever loved. He lifted his hand to her face, placed his fingers softly against her cheek.

She jumped, obviously startled, and Landon realized his error. She was blind; she couldn't see that he was going to touch her, and he'd scared her.

"Georgie, I'm sorry."

"No," she said, backing away. "Landon, please don't."

"Don't what?"

"Don't give me your pity. I can't take it." She shook her head. "Really, I can't."

"It isn't pity." What kind of number had Pete done on her? "I want to be your friend again. I want to help you. I care about you, Georgie. I always have, and I always will."

"I thought that I could do this, be around you again, but I can't." She quickly turned to leave the barn, but her foot slipped and she lost her balance. Landon moved toward her but wasn't fast enough, and she fell hard, her head popping solidly against one of the wooden stalls. She yelled, and Fallon reared up, spooked by the sudden scream.

"Let me help." Landon moved toward her, but she scurried backward like a trapped animal, her boots pushing frantically to edge as far away as possible.

"No, Landon," she said, her words sharp and clipped, and her eyes as wide as those of her spooked horse.

"Georgie, you're hurt."

"Leave, Landon. Please." She crawled up to her hands and knees, then awkwardly stood and put a hand to the back of her head.

He saw red seeping through her fingers and knew she'd cut her scalp. "Georgie, let me help."

"I. Said. No!"

Her mother entered the barn. "Georgiana?" She looked to Landon, gave him a regretful shake of her head.

"Mommy? Mommy, you okay? What's wrong?" Abi ran past her grandmother to get to her momma.

Georgiana blinked, moved her bloody hand to her face and rubbed her forehead.

"Oh, Mommy, you're bleeding!"

"Georgiana, what happened, honey?" Eden asked.

"She hit her head on the stall," Landon stopped talking when Eden held up her hand.

"It's okay, Georgiana," Eden soothed, inspecting the wound. "Not too bad at all. We'll get it cleaned up. Everything is going to be fine."

"I know where the medicine stuff is, Grandma," Abi said. "Remember, you showed me the other day. It's in the back bathroom, right?"

"Right, Abi. Why don't you help your mommy go to the house and hold one of those big square white bandages on it until I get there in a second, okay? That would really help Grandma and Mommy."

"I can do that." Abi took Georgiana's shaky hand and led her out of the barn.

"Momma," Georgiana said, her tone holding a subtle warning.

"I just want to tell Landon bye."

Georgiana left the barn with Abi without another word to Landon.

Eden waited until they were gone then looked

pointedly at him. "A lot has happened since she last saw you." Her lower lip quivered. "She isn't the same girl. She's doing much better, I think, but she won't ever be the same. It was bad enough that she went blind so soon after the marriage and while she was pregnant too. She was worried about being a good mother and about how she would take care of a baby without being able to see." Eden shook her head. "And somehow, Pete managed to make all of that worse. Oh, he never said anything negative in front of me, but Georgiana told me the things he'd say when I wasn't around. I've got to tell you, I wish she'd moved back here years ago, but she was so determined to save her marriage. She sure didn't want a divorce."

"She always said she'd marry for life."

"And she did. But Pete didn't. He married until trouble came, and then he was off with someone else in nothing flat." A tear slid down Eden's cheek. "I thought maybe if she came back here she'd find happiness again. And then, when I saw you, I thought you would be an important part of her finding it."

"But now?"

"I haven't given up on her, Landon. She's hiding. Hiding in this house and hiding from life. But she wants to make Abi happy. The only way we got her out of the house last night was because

Abi made her promise she'd go to town. But one time out every couple of months isn't living." She took a few steps to the end of the barn and peeked toward the house. "I should probably get in there and check on Abi's nursing skills."

"I would have tried to help her back then if I'd have known what happened, when she first lost her sight." He thought about her shoving away from him a moment ago. "I wish she'd let me help her now."

"I've been praying for Georgiana to find what she needs. She needs a friend, someone she can trust who can help her overcome the pain of her past. I honestly think you're the answer to my prayers. Don't give up on her, Landon."

"I won't." In fact, he would make sure Georgiana found a reason to live again. And if he had his way, a reason to love again.

Chapter Five

"Casey called me on my way home from the plant and said he's having dinner with Nadia's family. They wanted to do something special for him before he leaves Monday." John exited the house to find Landon grilling steaks on the back deck. "Hard to believe he's heading to college in just two days."

"Wish I'd have gotten a little more time with him before he leaves." Landon hadn't seen Casey at all today. His youngest brother had already headed out by the time he got back from Georgie's place this morning. Then Landon had kept himself occupied with work around the farm and with finalizing his plans for John throughout the day. Plus he'd gone to the feed store. If Casey had made a reappearance, he missed it. But Landon had wanted—needed—to stay busy. Anything to keep his mind off this morning's visit with Georgiana. All he wanted to do was go back over there and be with her, but he knew that wasn't what was best. He needed to give her time and perhaps give Eden time to talk to her and convince her to give Landon a chance to help her through her troubles. He planned to wait it out today, see Eden tomorrow at church and figure out where to go from here. In the meantime, he'd spend the evening catching up with his brother and eventually tell John what he'd done for him this afternoon.

"Well, I've got a pretty strong feeling Casey is gonna be coming home from school fairly often, not so much to see the two of us, but definitely to see Nadia," John said with a grin.

"You know, I bet you're right." Landon kept his tone normal and made certain his worry for Georgiana didn't show through.

John checked the abundance of meat on the grill. "Have mercy, how many people are you feeding? Did you invite Georgiana?"

"No, the visit this morning didn't go as well as I'd hoped." He could tell his brother that much.

"She and Pete are divorced though, right?"

"Yeah."

"He jumped ship when she lost her sight, huh?"

"Looks that way."

"Sounds like he's still the same ol' Pete we

knew in high school. Only wants something if it's perfect."

Landon nodded. Pete was their quarterback on the football team, and most of the school, and the town, thought he was downright amazing. But Landon and John had never been fooled. He was conceited, loved to party and was the most materialistic individual Landon had ever met. And he'd snowed Georgiana long enough for her to believe he'd really changed.

"Maybe Georgiana's still in shock from dealing with him. Probably needs a little time before talking to another member of the opposite sex, even if it's friendship." John shrugged. "That could be it. She'd have reason to be gun-shy if Pete did a number on her emotions."

"I'm going to try to talk to her again," Landon said. "Just giving her a little time first."

John nodded his head toward the meat. "So, if you didn't invite Georgiana—and a small army— who's gonna eat all of that?"

"I'd planned on Casey eating his share and then some, since he practically cleaned everyone's plates at Nelson's last night. But if he's eating with the Berrys, it looks like we're going to have some serious leftovers."

John grabbed a water bottle from the small fridge they kept on the deck. "Not a problem.

Steak and eggs are Casey's favorite for breakfast, so we'll give him a treat tomorrow morning before church."

"Steak and eggs work for me too," Landon said.

John still wore his work clothes from the steel mill, and Landon easily detected the metallic scent of the plant on the worn blue fabric. For some reason, John looked older than his twenty-eight years when he came home from the plant. It wasn't because the work was too hard for Landon's brother. There wasn't any kind of work more labor-intensive than farm work, but working on the farm was something John enjoyed. Landon knew his brother didn't enjoy working at the plant, but it was necessary. Or it had been for the past few years.

Not anymore.

But John didn't know that yet. In a few minutes though, he would. Landon felt great about what he'd accomplished today while John was gone. He glanced at his brother. John had donned his traditional Claremont baseball cap on the way home, and Landon was reminded of the fact that ten years ago, when John had played ball at the high school, he'd dreamed of having a better life. Going to college, getting a business degree and starting some type of business that would revolve around the farm and help the place thrive instead of merely survive.

Landon leaned against the porch railing near the grill. "I have something to talk to you about."

John sat in one of the rocking chairs lining the deck and took a long drink of water. Then he rubbed the back of his hand across his mouth and eyed his older brother. "More about Georgiana?"

"Nope."

"The farm? Because I had an idea today."

"I'm definitely interested in your idea, but this doesn't have to do with the farm. It's about you."

John's look turned curious. "All right, what's up?"

"You're only working at the steel plant now, right? No other jobs?"

John frowned. "Yeah, but not by choice. The feed store's sales dropped with livestock grazing more in the summer so they had to let me go. And the office supply store also cut half of their third-shift stockers, so I lost that one too. But I've applied to a couple of other places that may pan out. I can always swap to third shift at the plant if a day job opens up somewhere."

Landon would tell him what he learned at the feed store later. First things first. "You said you already saved enough for Casey's college expenses?"

"Yeah, I did. Not just me though; some of the money you sent every month went into that fund too." He locked eyes with Landon. "The money you sent really helped out. I don't know what we'd have done without it." He frowned. "I'd really hoped to get things in better shape before you got back."

Landon sent money every month, but if he'd realized how John had taken on extra jobs, he'd have sent more. Even so, he *had* saved the majority of his income while he was in the service and now thought it pretty bizarre how their thoughts had been so similar. He'd had a goal to help a brother as well.

"I did send *some* money," Landon said, "but I saved some too. And I saved it with a purpose in mind."

One of John's dark brows lifted. "What purpose?"

"The thing is, I want you to know how much I appreciate you working so hard to take care of Casey while I was gone and saving the money to pay for him to go to Alabama."

"You don't have to thank me," John said, clearly a little uncomfortable with the sentimental turn of the conversation. Not very guy-like to sit and talk about how thankful they were for each other. A decade ago they'd have merely shoved each other and let that be the extent of their brotherly expressions. But Landon had learned during his time in the service that sometimes you never got a chance to tell people, show people, how much they mean before they're gone. He wasn't going to make that mistake with his brother, and he definitely wasn't going to downplay everything John had done.

"I know I don't *have* to thank you, but I want to." Landon turned the meat, then closed the grill and moved to sit beside his brother. "And I want to do something else too, something I've planned for a while." He smiled. "About eight years of planning, actually. Something that involves you."

"Something you've been planning eight years that involves me? Should I be worried about whatever you're about to say?" John looked skeptical.

"Nah, I think you should be pretty happy about it." He'd looked forward to this conversation since the day he'd made the decision to help John out, and he couldn't wait to see how his brother reacted to the news.

John set his water bottle on the small wooden table by his rocker, inhaled deep and let it out. "Okay, I'm not sure what you're about to tell me, but let 'er rip. I'm ready."

Landon nodded, knowing John was indeed ready for the next stage in his life, a stage he should have entered about ten years ago. But the farm had been struggling financially then as well, and they'd had to take care of their mother during her depression. So John had given up on his dream.

But Landon hadn't.

"You know how you were working so hard and saving the money to pay for Casey to go to school," Landon started.

"Yeah," John said, and quickly added, "but I wanted to."

"I know that, and I admire it." If Landon couldn't already tell how uncomfortable John was with his gratitude, he'd have elaborated on how much he admired everything John had sacrificed to take care of Casey, but instead he said, "Well, like I said, I was saving too."

John's head tilted, causing his baseball cap to look a little lopsided. "Saving for…"

Landon smiled. "I was saving for you."

John blinked. "For me?"

"Yeah, and I kind of set it all in motion earlier today, so I hope that you'll want it as much as you used to."

Undeniably thrown, John asked, "Are you going to tell me what you've done or have I got to guess? 'Cause I have no idea what you're talking about."

"While you were saving for Casey's college education, I was saving for yours. I know you wanted to get a business degree and eventually run some kind of business that involved the farm, more than selling beef. And I want you to get that degree."

John's mouth dropped open and then he shook his head. "Dude, what'd you go and do?"

Landon laughed at the way John swiftly went back into high school conversation. Raising Casey had worn off on him more than he probably realized. "I registered you for classes at the college in Stockville. And I've saved enough for you to get a four-year degree too. I have enough for you to go pretty much anywhere you want, but I figured you'd probably want to stay near the farm. So I registered you at Stockville, just twenty minutes away. Classes start this week."

John's jaw clenched, and he pulled at his lower lip with his teeth. Landon knew the look. It was the same attempt to hide emotion that John had the day they lost their father. And again at their mother's funeral. John was pretty good at holding it all inside, but not good enough that Landon couldn't see that he was touched. Then John visibly swallowed and looked at Landon. "Man, I don't know what to say."

"You don't have to say anything." Landon stood, moved to the grill and returned his attention to the steaks. "But you do need to log in and finish the information on your student record. There were a few things I didn't know. You should have an e-mail with your log-in information."

"That would be awesome, really it would, man, but…" John shook his head. "I don't think I can. I mean, I can finish the student info, but I don't think I'm able to go back to school."

"Why not?" Landon hadn't anticipated John turning down his offer…at all. "It's what you've always wanted, right?"

"Yeah, yeah it is." His head continued to shake, and his mouth shifted to a frown. "But there's the farm. If you've got money saved, we should put it toward the loans, don't you think?"

Landon processed the main thing John still hadn't said, and it was time to get everything on the table and make a plan. "The farm—how bad is it?"

"The economy has killed us over the past few years. Beef sales have dropped, and I never was any good at crops. I tried it one year, but nothing yielded. I don't even know what I did wrong." He shook his head defeatedly. "I even tried fixing up all the old fishing shacks on the other end of the pastures, thought maybe I could rent them out, but I didn't have the funds to finish or to advertise." John inhaled thickly, blew it out. "I'm almost a year behind on everything. The bank's been lenient because of them knowing us and all, but they've done all they can. I think I was lucky to get six more months to catch up before they foreclose."

Landon felt like he was back in Afghanistan and the world was literally blowing up all around him. The situation was even worse than he'd realized, but he wasn't going to throw in the towel. And he wasn't going to give up on John's dream. "They *aren't* going to take it, and you *are* going back to school."

"I really think we should use that money you saved for my college to cover some back payments on the farm. I can go back to school later, but I really appreciate what you tried to do."

"Let me think a minute." Landon rubbed his head and concentrated on a strategy to tackle their problem. He rocked back and forth in the chair. *Come on, Lord. Help me know what we should do. We can't lose the farm, but I don't want to give up on John going back to school either. Help me, Lord.*

"Do you want to see the account statements? I have them in the kitchen." John stood and moved toward the door.

"Yeah, let me take a look at them." Within a couple of minutes, Landon held the statements for three loans, all fairly substantial and each nearly a year past due.

"I'm catching up, but like I said, I was behind already, and I was also saving for Casey's education." They sat for a moment in silence then John said, "I'll grab the steaks while you look those over." He got the meat from the grill and brought it inside, and Landon followed him into the house.

After filling their plates with steak, corn on the cob and baked potatoes, they sat at the wooden table that centered the kitchen and blessed their meal. John didn't say anything, but started eating. Landon, however, didn't lift a utensil. He sat back in his chair and ironed out his strategy.

Thank you, Lord. I think I've got it now.

"You going to eat?" John asked between bites.

"Yeah," Landon said with a grin. "I am. And you're going back to school." He cut into his steak, popped a big bite in his mouth and closed his eyes to enjoy the savory meat. "I tell you what, I didn't get food like this in the army."

Now John had stopped eating. "I'm going back to school? How you figure?"

"I'd saved enough to pay for four years. From what I saw on those statements, it'll take three years of it to get the majority of the back payments caught up. So I'll take care of doing that this week. You'll go ahead and start back to school and also start researching other ways the farm can earn more income. There've got to be other things we can do besides beef. I know a thing or two about crops, but it's too late for planting anything this season, so we'll have to plan that for next year. In the meantime, I already lined up a job off the farm."

"Already lined up a job? You've only been in town a day," John said, baffled.

"Had to go get feed today. When I got there, Mr. Ramer asked when you could start working again, because he had a guy quit and needed someone who can work the store and make deliveries." Landon grinned. "I told him you weren't available, but I was." He took a bite of potatoes. "I start Monday."

John couldn't contain his grin. "So you're gonna work at the feed store, and I'm going back to school?"

"That's the plan."

"And my first year of college is covered," John continued, obviously trying to follow the abundance of information Landon had spouted.

"Yeah, and we'll get the farm back on track enough that we'll be able to save that money for your next three years too," Landon said. "I want you to get that degree."

"Any idea how we'll go about doing that? Not getting me back to school but getting the farm back on track? You said the money you have saved will get the majority of the back payments. We've still got to get caught up and also make the payments the rest of the year, so that we're all caught up by the spring, if we don't want the bank to take everything."

"I figure you'll come up with an idea for how we'll do it. You're the one who'll be studying business. And you should only go to school and work on the farm. If you're going to do this right, you'll need time to study and time to iron out how we're going to implement some kind of business plan around here. You won't have time to work other jobs too."

"I can't give up the steel plant," John said flatly. "That's where I have mine and Casey's insurance covered, and honestly, that regular income has saved us over the past few years, even if it isn't all that much. I can easily swap to third shift, three days on and four days off. I can do that and go to school, no problem."

Landon took another bite of steak. "I really didn't plan on you working and going to school, but I suppose if you've been handling the farm and three jobs, then you can probably still pull off the steel plant."

"And it'll be worth it for that insurance," John said.

"Yeah, I suppose it will."

John stabbed a bite of steak and popped it in his mouth. "You sure about working at the feed store? I thought you were planning to come home and run the farm."

"You've worked three jobs, run the farm *and* raised Casey. Yes, I'm sure. It's my turn to do my part."

"And I'll go to school," John said, his desire to smile now almost breaking free. No doubt he was excited about the idea of getting that degree.

"Yeah, and make the most of it. We don't have long for you to find a way to put this place back in the black."

"You really think I can do that?"

"I know you can."

John swallowed thickly through the emotion. "I really appreciate this, Landon. I won't let you down, dude."

"I know you won't."

"You know, I did have an idea about something we could do at the farm. Read about it in one of the ranching magazines, but never really had the time to investigate it. Might be worth a shot, though."

"What is it?"

"Trail rides and campouts. Lot of ranches up in Tennessee and Kentucky are doing these tourist packages where you bring folks in and take them on trail rides through the mountains, set them up camping, things like that. I was thinking about all of the trails we have leading across Lookout Mountain and the campsite possibilities along the way. All of that land down by the Coosa River, you know, would be a good place for camping. And there's that trail by the old tree house that leads all the way to town. Maybe provide a day trip with something that involves the merchants at the square."

Landon's smile was instant. "Sounds good to me." He pointed his fork in John's direction. "And it also sounds like a business degree is going to suit you well."

John grinned back. "Yeah, I reckon it might." He had his phone on the table near his plate, and he tapped a few keys and scanned a few sites throughout dinner. Obviously, he was too excited about his new opportunity to wait until they finished eating.

Landon loved seeing him this anxious to start. "What sites are you checking out?"

"Other business ventures for a farm, besides livestock and crops."

"Such as?"

"It looks like the trail riding idea might be a good possibility. According to this site, recreation, tourism and woodlots are good alternate sources for income when the beef and produce industries are down." John glanced up. "We may be sitting on a tourist venture. Says here that dude ranches are still popular tourist attractions, especially if they let guests participate in the ranching. That's one way to get some help around the farm too. Have them pay for a vacation and then put them to work."

Landon laughed. "Somehow, I'm thinking folks would catch on to your ulterior motive before long, especially if you have them mucking out stalls."

"Probably so. But according to this, the nearest dude ranch is in North Georgia. There isn't a single one in Alabama. We'd be the first." John kept tapping keys. "Some go to ranches just to learn cowboy tricks."

Landon couldn't resist. "Do you *know* any cowboy tricks?"

"Not a single one," John said with a grin. "But I'm willing to learn for the betterment of our business."

It'd been a long time since Landon had felt so at ease, so at home. He'd missed this, visiting with John, more than he realized. And he needed it after what had happened this morning with Georgiana.

"Seriously, though, we could probably do something around here that's touristy. I don't know—" John winked "—but I'm sure I'll figure it out."

"That's what I'm counting on."

They finished dinner, cleaned up the mess in the kitchen and then headed out to the barn. As though Landon hadn't been gone, the two of them picked up with splitting the nightly chores. Feeding the horses, cleaning the stalls, checking on the cows, while John's hound dog Lightning dozed lazily in one corner of the barn.

"Funny, that's the first I've seen of Lightning since I got back," Landon said.

"Yeah, I should probably change his name to Drowsy," John said. "The vet keeps telling me he isn't sleeping."

"He isn't?"

"Nope. According to Doc Sheridan, he's on guard."

The old dog lifted one droopy eye, then plopped it back down in place.

Landon smirked. "He's a mighty quiet guard dog. Used to be, Lightning wouldn't have missed the fact that we were grilling steaks."

"He knows I'll bring some steak down here to him later, and he doesn't have to move." John squatted beside the old dog and rubbed behind his ears. Lightning made some kind of noise. There wasn't really a way to describe it, maybe half moan, half howl. "That means he likes this," John said.

"Glad you clarified."

His brother smiled broadly. "He gets excited every now and then. Loves to go along when I ride the ridge."

"He can keep up?" Landon asked.

"Okay, when I walk the ridge."

Landon nodded. "Now that I can see."

John left Lightning and moved to stand by Landon, giving Sam a molasses treat. "You're gonna spoil her."

"Says the guy feeding the hound dog rib eye."

John laughed. "So, you ready to talk about it?" He pulled a sprig of hay from a bale nearby, placed it in his mouth then shifted it to the side. "Seeing Georgiana?"

"What do you want to talk about? I told you it didn't go great, and I'm going to try again."

"Did you find out anything? About what happened with her and Pete? Was it the blindness?"

"I didn't find out much, except that she wanted me to leave," he said honestly.

"Ouch, that had to hurt. But you know, a lot has happened to her since you left. Marriage, blindness, a child...and then a divorce." John pulled the hay from his mouth. "Those kinds of things can change a person. And Daniel said she's been in Claremont a couple of months, but until last night, I hadn't seen hide nor hair of her around town, not even at church. I've seen her mom. Eden is always there, and I've even seen her daughter, but I didn't realize who she was at the time. Cute little girl."

"Who did you think she was?"

John shrugged. "I don't know. I guess I figured it was one of the kids that took riding lessons from Eden. But anyway, Georgiana doesn't come with them to church. And that's not the girl we used to know."

"No, it isn't," Landon said. "But like you said, she's been through a lot. And last night I wasn't the only one who hadn't heard about her blindness. Daniel knew because of Mandy taking Abi's pictures, but none of the other guys. Maybe she's stayed at their farm because she wasn't ready for everyone to see her that way."

"Maybe," John said, nodding his head and also rubbing Sam's neck, since Sam acted like she was totally starved for affection, nudging them nonstop as they stood at her stall. Landon knew John and Casey had been great to his horse while he was away, but obviously Sam hadn't forgotten her owner. Landon smiled at that. When something means enough, it isn't forgotten.

Why had Georgie forgotten that he used to be able to help her through tough times?

"It seems odd that she has been next door for that long and I haven't even seen her. Then again, way back when, I'd see her at church and school,

nd of course riding the ridge every afternoon
vith you. Since she isn't coming to church and
ince we aren't in school, that knocks those two
ut. And we wouldn't see her riding. I mean, blind
olks can't ride, right?"

Landon's brows lifted. Georgiana had been with
'allon when he arrived this morning, and he'd seen
er caressing her beloved friend. Landon hadn't
een the only one close to Georgiana; Fallon had
oo. Maybe through Fallon, Landon could find his
vay back to Georgiana's heart as well. "I have no
dea if blind folks can ride or not." He gave Sam
ne last pat before he left the barn and returned
o the house. He suddenly wanted to surf the Net
nd get some answers. "But I believe I can eas-
ly find out." And if blind people could ride, then
Landon had to find a way to make that happen…
or the beautiful blind woman that so completely
eld his heart.

Chapter Six

Landon was fairly accustomed to going withou
sleep in Afghanistan, so staying up the majority
of Saturday night researching horse riding for the
blind hadn't been difficult. However, he couldn'
deny his eyes had a hint of sleep-deprivation sting
as he left the church after the morning service. Bu
he didn't rush out and head home for a Sunday af
ternoon nap. Instead he scanned the congregation
exiting the building until he spotted Eden.

She shook Brother Henry's hand, then started
down the stairs toward the parking lot, but stopped
when she saw Landon leaning against a large oak
tree near the playground. He held up a hand, and
she smiled and walked toward him as though she
totally expected to find him waiting for her after
the service. Abi was at her grandmother's side
chatting nonstop, her red curls bouncing along
with every syllable.

"I thought I'd probably see you here this morning," Eden said.

Abi noticed that her grandmother's attention had turned to someone else, and she looked up to see Landon. "Oh, hey, Mr. Landon!" She peered past him. "Did you ride your horse to church?"

"Nah, I brought the truck. Not as much fun, but it gets me around. How's your momma's head today?" Landon directed the question to Abi, even though Eden could probably give him a more detailed answer. He could tell the little girl loved her mother and probably wanted to be the authority on all things Georgiana.

"She's fine. I took her to the medicine stuff like Grandma said, and we put a big square white patch on it, but then when Grandma came in, she looked at it real good and said it just needed a little Band-Aid instead of that big one. I knew how Mommy likes Little Mermaid, and so I got a Little Mermaid one and we put it on. It has Ariel on it, and she's holding a fork, cause she thought it was a comb. It was her treasure. The Band-Aid stuck to Mommy's hair a little, but I couldn't figure out how to not get it to stick to that too if we needed it to stick to the hurt spot," she said, shrugging her shoulders, then tilting her head at Landon. "You haven't seen Little Mermaid, have you?"

He fought the urge to laugh at her excited chatter of information. "I'm afraid not."

"Ariel's a mermaid with pretty red hair like Mommy's hair. That's why I like her, and 'cause my hair is red too. And it's okay that you haven't seen it. Sometimes boys don't see all the good movies, because they're boys. But you should see that one, 'cause it's got boy stuff too." Her mouth quirked to the side and strawberry brows furrowed for a moment while she apparently thought about something, then her mouth perked up in a smile and she said, "Sebastian is a boy."

"Sebastian?"

"Uh-huh, he's Ariel's friend the red crab. He's smart about the ocean stuff, but mostly he's her best friend and—" she shook her head "—you really need to see it. It's a lot to explain."

"But trust me, she'll be happy to provide every detail if you give her time," Eden said. "Our little Abi is a talker."

"That's what Mommy says too." Abi smiled, sending a waterfall of copper freckles dancing across her cheeks.

Landon was drawn to the precious, energetic child.

Eden smiled at her granddaughter, then glanced up at Landon. "Were you wanting to talk to me privately, Landon?"

He nodded. "I wondered if Abi might want to spend a little time on the playground for a few minutes while we chat."

"Does that sound good to you, Abi?" Eden asked. "I see Autumn and Nathan are playing."

"Sure! But someone has to hold my sun catcher." She held up the craft she'd made in Sunday school.

"I'd be happy to," Landon said, accepting the beaded square, then watching her run toward the playground, her feet kicking up wood chips as she darted toward a merry-go-round where several other kids were playing.

"That girl has more energy than Georgiana and I put together. I've gotta tell you, I've been sleeping real good at night since they came to live with me. Abi wears me out—" she laughed "—but in a good way."

"She looks like Georgiana."

Eden nodded. "Just like her, doesn't she? I remind Georgiana of that all the time."

"Georgiana doesn't come to church with y'all?"

She shook her head. "She's still as close to God as she ever was, maybe even closer. Listens to the Bible and devotionals on CD every day. But she isn't ready for all of this yet, being around people that knew her before her blindness." She swallowed, turned her gaze from Abi to Landon. "I'm hoping that she'll work up to church again eventually, but we'll take it a step at a time." She sighed. "I know she felt terrible about what happened at the barn, Landon."

"I'm sure she didn't feel nearly as badly as I did. She got hurt. I didn't. I wasn't even thinking about the fact that she couldn't see me reaching for her. I'm sure it's scary when someone touches you and you aren't expecting it."

"That's true, but I hope what happened yesterday won't keep you from visiting her at the farm. Like I told you before, she could really use a friend."

"I've been thinking about that ever since I left yesterday morning, about a way that I can help Georgiana. She hardly has any interaction with anyone anymore, does she?"

"No, she doesn't. The other night, when Abi and I talked her into going to the town square to buy a new dress and shoes, that was the first time Georgiana has left the farm since they moved here. She's working full time, but she can work from the farm, so she really never has a reason to leave the house."

"Georgie's working?" He hadn't considered that she might have a job. What type of job would she have?

Eden nodded. "She's a medical transcriptionist. Her friend Linda helped her get the job in Tampa, and the doctors there have been so pleased with her work that they told her she could continue to do their transcription after she moved back to Alabama. It's really been a blessing for Georgiana, makes her feel as though she can still accomplish something." Eden nodded her approval at Abi as she circled the merry-go-round.

"So she doesn't leave the farm," Landon said, remembering the vibrant, fun girl of his youth and trying to reconcile that to the woman currently shutting herself off from the world.

Eden's lips pinched together, as though she were deciding how much to say. "She is planning to attend Abi's piano recital in a few weeks. Abi really wants her to go, and Georgiana wants to be a real mother to Abi, in spite of her blindness. The trip to the town square was kind of a test run to get ready for that recital."

"Do you think she'll be able to go?"

Eden released another heavy sigh. "I honestly don't know, but I hope so, for Abi's sake."

"Well, I thought of something that might help Georgiana and that I think she'd really enjoy. It wouldn't require her to leave the farm, so we wouldn't have to worry about that for now."

"What is it?" Eden asked, her curiosity obviously piqued at the possibility of something that could help her daughter.

"Fallon. Georgie was always happiest when she was riding. I thought maybe if I helped her to get closer to Fallon again, to actually ride Fallon the way she used to, then maybe that would be a way to make her feel she can accomplish something again, that she can enjoy life again."

"Oh, she wanted to ride again. She asked Pete about boarding a horse in Tampa so she could ride."

Landon was surprised. "She wanted to ride? Why didn't she?"

"Pete convinced her there was no purpose to her riding again, that it was merely a way for her to get hurt. Something like that. Georgiana never told me, you see, but once when I was down there visiting, I asked if she would like for me to send Fallon to Tampa, told her they could board her and she could ride again. There's no reason a blind person shouldn't be able to ride, you know."

"I know." He'd researched it, in fact, most of the night.

"But Pete simply said no, and that was that."

Eden gazed at the playground, but Landon could tell she was thinking about what he'd suggested, him helping Georgiana to ride Fallon again. If he could give her back the enjoyment, the freedom, of riding her favorite horse again, he thought that might also break through the barrier she had with Landon.

"What do you think?" he asked.

"I've thought about getting her to ride again myself. I even asked her about it a couple of times since she moved back home."

"What did she say?"

"That she would be too afraid of the unknown, afraid of what she wouldn't be able to see while riding. Fallon is the gentlest horse around, but every horse can get spooked occasionally, and every horse can feel its rider's fears. She didn't know how Fallon would handle it if she was obviously afraid."

"I spent a lot of time reading about equine therapy for the blind last night, and I think it'd be great for Georgiana. I could help her get over that fear of the unknown, be right there with her every step of the way." Landon's excitement at the possibility picked up his tone. "It would actually be much easier for her because she was an accomplished rider already. There wouldn't be nearly as much to learn. Instead, she'd only need to remember."

"That does sound like a good idea, but Georgiana has a lot of fears to conquer now. And I'm not certain that's the first one that needs to be tackled," Eden said.

"Georgiana's too young and way too beautiful to hide from life," Landon said.

Eden looked touched by his words. "She is, isn't she? I'd thought she'd eventually break out of her shell a bit here, back where she grew up, but she hasn't."

"I want to help her ride again," Landon said, more resolutely than before. "She always seemed so free, so happy when we'd ride the ridge and the trails, and I want to see her smile like that again, want to hear her laugh that way again."

"Oh, I would love to see that too." Eden closed her eyes for a moment, and Landon suspected she was remembering the vision of her daughter riding Fallon through the fields.

"Then there's one more thing I'd like to ask you to help me with, if you don't mind," he said.

She opened her eyes. "What's that?"

"Could you talk to her, try to get her thinking about the possibility of riding again, and I guess more importantly about the possibility of letting *me* help her ride again?"

He knew how much Georgiana had always valued her mother's opinion, and from the way she'd bolted away from him yesterday, it'd be difficult for Landon to get close enough to talk her into spending one-on-one time with him while he helped her ease back into riding. But that's what he wanted, one-on-one time with Georgiana. Time to grow close again. Time to help her find freedom again. Time for her to perhaps find their friendship again. And, if Landon's dreams could come true, to find more…with him.

"Will you talk to her for me?" he repeated.

She smiled broadly. "Of course I will."

Chapter Seven

Abi tapped Georgiana's arm. "Momma, are you done working yet?"

"I'm not completely done." Georgiana turned off the Dictaphone and removed her headset so she could hear her daughter better. "But I can finish later on. Did you want to talk to me?"

Abi huffed out an exasperated breath. "No, but Grandma is still at the grocery store, and I don't want to watch TV, and I've practiced my piano until my fingers hurt, and it's pretty outside, and I'm bored." She was usually fairly good at entertaining herself, but the summer was drawing to a close, and she'd exhausted all of the solo entertainment options for a six-year-old. She was too young to venture off by herself any farther than the barn, and she'd evidently had enough of the house and the barn for today.

"You're bored?" Georgiana wrapped the cord

around the headset and placed it on top of the Dictaphone player.

"Yep. Can we do something fun? Not just in the house or at the barn. Let's go somewhere different."

"Go somewhere different?" Georgiana couldn't "go" anywhere. She couldn't drive, and Abi was quite familiar with that limitation. "Where do you want to go?"

"You said you did fun stuff here when you were little. You did hikes and fishing and climbing trees and stuff. That's what you said we could do when we moved here, but we haven't done *any* of that yet."

Georgiana frowned. Her daughter was right. She'd played up the farm and all of the wonderful things it had to offer so Abi wouldn't be too upset about moving, but then she hadn't made an effort to help her little girl do anything more than the horse-riding lessons. And, if she were being completely honest, *she* wasn't the one doing that for her daughter; Abi's grandmother was. "We do need to do something fun, don't we?"

"Yep, we do."

"You have anything in mind?"

"We could walk to the pond." Abi's voice sounded so hopeful that Georgiana felt badly for not "doing something fun" before now.

"Walk to the pond? That's what you want to do?" The pond was a fairly long distance from the house, practically at the other end of their property, but Georgiana thought it'd do her good to get out and get some fresh air with Abi while they journeyed across the pasture and enjoyed the pretty day. "You know what, that does sound fun."

"But let's don't *just* walk. Let's put the rocks on the pond the way Grandma was talking about the other night at dinner. Remember?"

Georgiana did remember. Eden told Abi about how Georgiana had been a pro at skipping stones when she was a little girl, and she'd said that they would have to go to the pond and see if Abi had inherited that talent. But she'd been talking about teaching Abi herself. How would Georgiana skip stones or teach her daughter to do it if she couldn't see?

"Remember?" Abi repeated.

"Yes, I do." There was no way Georgiana could turn her down. *Somehow* she had to accomplish the task of skipping rocks blind.

"Let's go do that, okay? Grandma has rocks in her flower bed. I can get some, and you can teach me how to make them walk on water."

Georgiana laughed. "Skip on water. That's what you do, make them skip across the top of the water." She remembered how much fun she and Landon always had trying to see whose rock could go the farthest. He always won, but she gave him a good run for the money.

"Okay, skip on the water." Abi hugged Georgiana, then ran across the room. Georgiana heard the door leading outside creak open. "I'll go get the rocks. What kind do we need?"

"Small, flat ones. About the size of a quarter, or a little bigger. Those will work best." Georgiana started toward the door. "I'll help you get some good ones."

"Awesome! This will be so much fun!" Abi's footsteps pounded the front porch and then Georgiana heard tumbling rocks as she apparently searched through the flower beds that spanned the length of the house. "Is this one good?" Abi ran to Georgiana and put a smooth flat stone in her palm.

"That one is perfect."

"Okay. How many more?" Abi asked.

"Fill your pockets, and I'll fill mine too. But not too many to make your jeans heavy when we walk." Georgiana wasn't sure how many it would take for her to get the hang of skipping stones again, or if she'd even be able to accomplish the task when she couldn't see the water. But she desperately wanted to do something with her daughter, and since she was still skittish about doing anything that required leaving the farm, she really needed to find some "fun stuff" for them to do on the property. Skipping stones would be the first step, and she was glad to hear Abi so excited about doing the simple excursion together.

God, this isn't something that I'd typically pray for, but I know all things are possible with You. So today, if it be Your will, let at least one of my stones find its way across the top of the water before it sinks.

They walked for at least twenty minutes with Georgiana letting Abi tug her in the right direction. Oh, she knew her way around the farm, but the open fields were a little more difficult to navigate with the occasional small hills and valleys along the way. Abi chatted nonstop, and Georgiana reveled in the sound of her daughter's enthusiasm. She was so much like Georgiana had been at that age, full of energy and seeing every day as a potential adventure.

Georgiana had thought her whole life would be that way, one big adventure after another. But now she rarely even left her home. And her daughter was over-the-moon excited about Georgiana joining her for a walk to a pond and an attempt at skipping stones.

Suddenly, Abi's happiness hit Georgiana for what it was—anticipation of actually doing something with her mom, just the two of them making the day special by simply being together. Abi would undoubtedly want to go lots of places, do lots of things, with her momma. There would be field trips and school plays and festivals. And Georgiana wanted to be there.

God, please, help me get past this rut. Help me to stop being afraid, Lord. For Abi...and for me.

"There it is! The pond!" Abi yanked on Georgiana's arm and picked up her pace until they were practically running across the field.

"Abi, you'd better tell me when we're getting close, or I may go toppling right in," Georgiana said breathlessly as they ran.

Abi giggled and slowed her run to a trot. "Okay, okay," she said, still laughing, "we can slow down. It's right there."

Georgiana may not have been able to see it, but she could sense the water ahead. She could hear the liquid gently moving against the edge of the pond. Crickets chirped loudly, and at least one frog attempted to give them some competition in the noise department. She inhaled thickly, enjoyed the clean, crisp air filling her lungs, then exhaled. "It's nice here, isn't it?"

"It's prettier than the beach," Abi said, which was huge by Abi standards. She'd loved the beach in Tampa and was hesitant to move to a place without sand, even if it was where her grandma lived. But Georgiana could hear the sincere appreciation of the farm's beauty in her daughter's voice, and it touched her heart.

She visualized the large pond, its moss-covered bank and occasional wild clover blooming along the edge. "I always thought it was prettier than a beach too." Georgiana had never wanted to move to Tampa, but she'd been willing to for Pete. And she'd stayed there trying to make their marriage work. But Claremont was home.

A fairly loud splash sounded nearby. "Abi? Did you throw a rock already?"

"No, but I saw that. It was a fish! Did you hear how big a splash he made? Oh, look, another one splashed over there!"

Georgiana nodded. Her father had stocked the pond when she was little, and apparently the fish still thrived. "I'd forgotten about how many fish are in this pond. We'll have to come out here and fish sometime too."

"Nah, I don't think I want to," Abi said. "We'd have to touch them, wouldn't we?"

Georgiana grinned. "Assuming we caught some, then yes, we would. And we'd have to bait hooks as well."

"Definitely don't want to do that," Abi said. "We can just throw our rocks."

"Yeah, I guess fishing might not be all that appealing for a girl if you have to bait your own hook and touch anything you caught." Georgiana's father had always done both for her during their trips to the pond. She hated that Abi didn't have a man in her life to do those kind of things. She'd have her weekend with Pete every month, but Georgiana was certain Pete wasn't a "take his daughter fishing" kind of guy. She couldn't even recall whether Pete liked fishing.

The thought of another guy, one who loved the outdoors, came to mind, but she shook the image away. Chances were she wouldn't see Landon Cutter again after the way she'd run away from him Saturday.

Stones clunked together loudly, and Georgiana could tell Abi was in the process of emptying her pockets. She tucked away the unpleasant memory of leaving Landon in the barn and concentrated on enjoying this time with her daughter.

"I've got my rocks ready," Abi said. "What do I do now?"

Georgiana slipped her hand in her own pocket and withdrew a slick rock about the size of a half dollar. She rubbed it between her thumb and first two fingers and then eased one foot ahead of her to see how close she stood to the water's edge.

When her foot found air fairly quickly, she gasped. "We're right by the water."

"I thought that's where we were supposed to be," Abi said.

Georgiana took a step back, reached her hand out and made sure Abi moved back too. "Yes, but not quite that close," she said. "Right here should be fine."

"Okay, so what do I do?" Abi asked.

Georgiana turned to the side, rubbed the smooth stone again, and then did her best to flick her wrist sideways as she pivoted and released the stone toward the water.

She wanted to hear the *pit-pit-pat* of a stone hitting the surface in intervals. Instead she heard one solid *plunk*. "Oh, what did it do?"

"It fell in," Abi said. "That's not the way Grandma said it works. That didn't even kind of look like walking on water."

"No, I suppose it didn't." Maybe she sent the rock out with too much of an arch instead of flat above the water. Without being able to see, she had no way of viewing the water's surface, no way to know how to gauge when the stone would hit or how hard. So she focused on listening, hearing the liquid against the bank and determining about how far she should attempt to send the rock out to get it started on its journey. "I'm going to try again."

She listened, turned, twisted her wrist and flicked it toward the water.

After a pause that seemed to go on forever, she heard a beautiful *pit-plunk*.

"Mom! I think you did it. It bounced before it dropped."

Georgiana laughed. "So it skipped once. Good deal. Come here, and I'll show you how to do it, then you can try too. And I will see if I can get it to take more steps."

Abi situated herself in front of Georgiana and let her mother wrap an arm around her to show her how to hold the stone.

"Gently in your fingers, like this. And then you're going to turn your wrist, kind of quick, like this." She moved Abi's wrist. "You've got it?"

"Yep, I'm ready."

"Okay, flick your wrist toward the water, and when your stone is going that direction then you let it go. You kind of pretend like you are pushing it out over the top of the water, or that's how I did it when I was your age. Now I have to dream how I want it to work, but back then, I could look at the water and tell where I needed the stone to go." She had no idea if her words were making sense, and since she couldn't see Abi's expression, she was unable to tell whether her daughter understood. "You get it?"

"I think so."

"Want me to guide your hand the first time?"

"Sure."

Georgiana wrapped her palm around Abi's hand then helped her make the motion with her wrist. The stone made a solid *thunk* when it hit the water.

Abi grunted. "Nope, that wasn't it."

"It takes a little time to get the feel of it," Georgiana said, and then put another stone in Abi's hand. "Let's keep trying."

"O-kay." Abi tossed three more stones straight to the bottom, then she stepped away from her mom. Georgiana heard her collapse against the grass. "I'm *never* gonna get it."

"Sure you will. It just takes a little practice. Let's not give up, okay?"

"You do another one, and then I'll try again," Abi said.

Georgiana withdrew another smooth stone from her pocket, followed the same motions as before and sent it toward the water to hear *pit-pit-pit-plunk.* "Yes!" she cheered, clapping her hands together.

Abi had obviously gotten back to her feet. "You did it! You did it, Momma!" She grabbed Georgiana in a hug.

"So now you try again," Georgiana said. "Because, like Grandma said, you've surely got the talent too." She sat on the grass and listened to her daughter.

Abi sent two more stones in without any success. "I *can* do it."

Georgiana loved hearing confidence in her little girl's tone. "Of course you can."

Then with a grunt, Abi sent another stone sailing.

Pit-pit-pit-pit-plunk!

Abi cheered, and Georgiana jumped up to celebrate. Unfortunately, she hadn't realized that as she moved around near the bank, she'd evidently moved closer to the edge. Her feet hit the mossy side and the next thing she knew…she was in. Completely. And wet. Completely.

"Mom!" Abi yelled. "Mom, are you okay?"

Georgiana came up out of the water laughing. "I'm—fine." She pushed her way up to the grass, then pulled her heavy, jean-clad legs around the edge. "I guess in the future I should pay closer attention to where the water is before I start celebrating your rock walking on water, huh?"

Laughing, Abi plopped down beside Georgiana and hugged her. "Yes, you should! Oh, you're all muddy," she said, with an *ew* factor underlying each word.

Georgiana pushed her wet hair away from her

face and actually felt a little mud against her forehead. "I'm a mess, aren't I?"

Laughing, Abi pulled something—probably
grass—out of Georgiana's hair. "Yeah, Momma,
you are a mess."

"Wait till you tell your grandma!" Georgiana's
laughter rang out, and she was overcome with how
wonderful it felt to really laugh again. When was
the last time she'd laughed? "Oh, Abi, thank you."

Still giggling, Abi asked, "For what?"

"For being bored today and for getting me out
of the house to have fun."

"We should do this again tomorrow!"

Georgiana smiled. "I think we will, except tomorrow I'll try not to get so excited when you skip
your stones, and I'll plan to stay dry."

"Okay!" Abi clapped her hands together. "Aren't
you glad we didn't give up?"

Georgiana smiled. "Yes." Very glad.

"I still have six more to throw," Abi said. "Can
I throw them now, or do you need to go back and
take a bath or something?"

Georgiana laughed so hard she snorted. "No,
I can wait until you toss the rest of them, if you
can put up with looking at me all dirty. Here."
She emptied her pockets. "Throw these as well.
I'm done."

They stayed at the pond long enough for Abi to

successfully skip several more stones, then headed back toward the house. And since they'd been having so much fun, laughing and skipping rocks, Georgiana didn't notice the sound of the truck that headed up the driveway. Nor did she realize that a muscled cowboy was busy working in her barn… and hoping to catch a glimpse of Georgiana.

Landon wouldn't have to worry about finding a gym where he could work out now that he was back in Claremont. Every day provided enough physical activity for a week. In fact, he'd wager he was getting more exercise now than he did in the service. He'd been making deliveries for the feed store nonstop from the time he arrived early this morning until the end of the day, which meant he'd hauled fifty pound sacks of feed and more hay bales than he could count…from the time he arrived early this morning until the end of the day. And when he returned home, he'd need to get everything done around his own farm.

Definitely plenty of exercise.

His shirt and jeans were stuck to him from sweat, the muscles in his back stung. And his arms hadn't hurt this bad since he was a private doing PT and running the cinder track by the barracks…carrying twenty-five gallon jugs of water until he dropped.

And he felt great.

John had called to let him know how his first classes had gone at Stockville and also said that he was already making progress on the dude ranch idea. Landon had set up an appointment to meet with Andy Cothran at the bank tomorrow to discuss the farm loans and pay what he could on the back payments. And then his last scheduled delivery of the day was to the Sanders farm.

Things just kept getting better.

In fact, the only disappointing aspect to his day was when he arrived at the Sanders place and found it empty. Eden had said that Georgiana wouldn't leave the farm and that her only time out had been when they went to the square Friday night, but she must have left today. Landon wanted her to start getting out, but he had really hoped he'd see her when he made this delivery.

He unloaded the bags of feed and hay bales that Eden had ordered and stacked them in the barn while Fallon nickered from her stall.

"All right," he said, walking toward the burlap sack hanging near the tack room, "I bet I know what you want." He reached in and withdrew a green Granny Smith apple, then brought it to the mare. Fallon chomped noisily on the treat. "So, where'd your pretty owner go?" he asked, as though the horse could provide an answer.

Fallon, of course, didn't respond. But Landon did get an answer when he heard a child's voice, followed by the throaty laughter that never failed to warm his heart.

"You're gonna need a long bath!" Abi giggled through her words as she and Georgiana walked from the pasture toward the house. "A *very* long bath."

"You can stop telling me how messy I am. Trust me, I get it." Georgiana ran a hand down the side of her face and squished up her nose. "I'm pretty sure the mud has dried on."

Abi laughed. "Yep, you're gonna have to really scrub to get it off. Hey, I'm gonna get some lemonade. All that walking made me thirsty. Are you thirsty too? Want me to fix you some?"

"Sure, but I'm gonna stop and check on Fallon before I come in. I'll be there in a minute, okay?"

"Okay." Abi ran toward the house without a second glance toward the inside of the barn, where Landon watched the exchange between mother and daughter.

Georgiana wore a T-shirt that was pink, he thought, though it was hard to tell because it appeared to be covered in mud. Her jeans were rolled up to her calves and were also coated in what looked like caked mud. And as she walked closer, he saw her hair was damp and it looked like a sprig of grass had taken residence above her right ear.

She looked adorable.

Landon wanted to ask her what had happened, but he didn't want to scare her again, so he had to do something to let her know he was in the barn. He cleared his throat, and she stopped walking.

"Who's there?" A slight tremor quivered through her voice.

"It's me, Georgie."

"Landon?" Her hand moved to her hair, pushed it away from her face and caused the grass sprig to shift a little. "I—didn't know you were coming over."

"I'm actually making a delivery," he said. "I started working at the feed store today, and your mom's order was the last on my list before I head home." He took a step toward her, but then stopped when he remembered what had happened Saturday. "Georgie, I'm sorry about scaring you the other day. I wasn't thinking."

"It wasn't your fault," she said, her mouth easing to the side. "It's my problem." She turned her head toward the field and added, "I want to get better, though, for Abi. She wants me to be involved, wants me to have fun with her, but it's still hard."

"She looked like she was having fun just now." Landon suspected Eden hadn't yet talked to Georgiana about the possibility of her riding again, and he really wanted to give her a chance to think about it before he brought it up. But if he could get Georgiana to ride again, that would be another way she and Abi could enjoy time with each other and, if things went the way he planned, with him.

"She was, but she wants to do more than things around the farm. She wants me to go places with her, but it's still difficult. I feel people staring, and I don't want to do anything to embarrass her." She looked again toward the field, and one corner of her mouth lifted. "But we did have a good time together, and I want to have more times like that."

"Georgie, I want to help you—" Fallon snorted, then made a high-pitch whistling sound that Landon knew meant fear. Landon stopped talking and saw what had spooked the mare, a slight movement near Georgiana's foot. He focused on the image and prayed it wasn't what he thought, but the light brown markings on the coiled snake were clear. "Georgie." He kept his voice low and steady, and he could tell that she realized something wasn't right.

"What is it?" she whispered, her fingers opening at her side as though she knew something dangerous was near.

It was. Very near, in fact. Coiled and eyeing her exposed calf, and ready to strike.

"Dear God, help me," she whispered. "Landon, what is it? A snake? It's a snake, isn't it?"

He moved slowly to the side, picked up a shovel propped against the tack-room wall. "Stay still, Georgie."

"What kind?" she whispered, then her mouth clamped shut and she pinched her eyes together like someone bracing for the worst, which was what she would get if that snake hit his mark.

"Copperhead. Don't. Move." He eased toward the snake with the same slow, silent steps he'd often used when approaching an enemy camp and wished the thing was farther from her leg. There was no doubt it could reach her with ease, but Landon was determined to reach it first.

Help me, Lord. I can't miss.

Making certain not to make any jerking movements, he slowly raised the shovel, said one more quick prayer, then slammed it down solidly on his venomous target.

Georgiana's hand moved to her throat. "You got it?" she whispered. "Landon? Landon?"

"I got it." With adrenaline burning fiercely through his veins, he removed the dead snake from the barn, then returned to find Georgiana holding on to the rail and shaking her head. "What—what if Abi would have come in here with me?"

"I wouldn't have let it hurt her," Landon said.

Her head shook, and her eyes continued to blink. Her breathing was raspy, and Landon knew she was scared. She was probably thinking the same thing as Landon—*but what if he hadn't been here?* She had no way of seeing the danger.

The urge to protect her was so strong that Landon had to force himself to remain grounded to his spot and not wrap her in his arms and never let her go. But the image of her backing away from him Saturday kept him at bay.

"You're okay, Georgie. Everything's okay." He was so close, and she was trembling. He simply wanted to—had to—hold her and make sure she was all right. But he didn't want to frighten her again. "Georgiana, can I hold you?"

Her nod was subtle, but Landon didn't wait for anything more. He circled her in his arms and pulled her against his chest. "It's okay." Landon did his best to soothe her fear away, holding her close, telling her that the danger had passed.

"Thank you," she whispered, her words muffled against his chest. "I don't know what I'd have done."

He reflexively squeezed her tighter to his heart and thanked God that He'd put Landon here today at just the right time. *Let me always protect her, Lord. Let her begin to trust again. And, please, God, let her trust me again.*

Eden's car passed by the barn on her way to the house, and Georgiana straightened, then slowly stepped out of his embrace.

"We'll need to tell her about the snake," she said, "so she can keep an eye out for more."

Landon would keep an eye out too. In fact, he'd do everything he could to protect her from snakes and from anything else that might harm her.

"Landon?" Eden called as she stepped into the barn. "Oh, Georgiana," she said. "I didn't know you were here too." Her eyes widened as she took in their appearance. "Goodness, what happened to you two? You're both so, well, filthy."

Landon took in their appearance and realized her description was undeniably accurate. "Well, I'm actually here delivering your feed. I started working for the feed store today, and so I'll be making your deliveries now." He thumbed his shirt. "That's why I look like this." Then he realized Georgie had let him hug her, against his chest no less, when he was covered in sweat and grime. And yet she hadn't seemed anything but content in his arms. He looked back at her, and for the first time really noticed that she was almost completely coated in dried mud. He smiled. "I haven't really found out why Georgiana looks like that."

Her face was still tense from the close call with the copperhead, but at Landon's words, she found a smile. "I'd almost forgotten, with everything else that happened," she said, "but Abi and I went to the pond to practice skipping rocks."

"You did?" Eden beamed at her daughter. "Oh, that's wonderful, Georgiana. I'm sure Abi loved that."

"She did, especially when I started celebrating her stone skipping and was closer to the edge than I realized and fell in."

Eden's hand went to her mouth to contain her laugh, but it still escaped. And Landon didn't attempt to hide his.

"*That's* how you got so dirty?" he asked.

Georgiana nodded. "But we still had fun."

"I'm sure you did," Eden said, then she tilted her head. "What did you mean 'with everything else that happened'? What else happened?"

"Landon just killed a copperhead, and from the sound of things, it was about to strike...me."

Eden's eyes found Landon's and silently asked if Georgiana's thoughts were true. He nodded.

"Oh, my," Eden whispered. "You killed it, Landon?"

"I did."

"Thank you." Her voice was an emotional whisper.

"Mom! Your ice is all melting in your lemonade! Are you coming?" Abi yelled from the house.

"I forgot all about the lemonade." Georgiana still stood fairly close to Landon, and she seemed to sense his proximity, because she edged a little closer, whispered, "Thank you, again, Landon," and then turned and left the barn.

Eden waited until she'd reached the house then said, "I can't thank you enough, Landon."

"I'll help you keep an eye out for more copperheads," he said. "I didn't tell Georgiana, but I'll admit it to you. I was scared when I saw that snake so close to her leg."

"It was close?"

He nodded. "Too close."

"God sent you here to rescue her," Eden said, nodding as though she was certain of the fact.

"I was actually thinking the same thing a minute ago. I really want to help her, more than protecting her from snakes."

"She's going to be okay, Landon. I know she is. Walking to the pond and skipping rocks with Abi was a good start. And I think you were right about getting her to ride Fallon." She glanced at the palomino. "I haven't had a chance to talk to her about it yet, but I plan to later tonight." She gave him a slight smile. "She's starting to trust you again, I think. And after what Pete put her through, that's a miracle in itself."

Landon wanted to see if she said more about Pete, but she didn't, and he didn't ask.

She sighed. "I'd better go start unloading the car. Need to get my groceries put away."

"Want some help?"

"Nah, you've obviously been working hard all day. You go on home. I can handle it." She took a couple of steps, then turned back toward Landon. "And Landon, when I said that I thought God sent you here to rescue her, I wasn't just talking about the snake." She gave him another nod, then left the barn.

Chapter Eight

Landon had thought his meeting with Andy Cothran would take fifteen minutes tops; he'd been in the bank over an hour. Thankfully, Mr. Ramer understood that he needed to take care of the family's financial affairs and had told him not to worry about missing some time at the feed store while he went to the bank. But missing an hour of deliveries was the least of Landon's problems. Getting the bank on board with their business plan was at the top of the list.

Then again, according to Andy, they didn't have any hint of a business plan, just an idea that was too far-fetched for the bank to approve. Andy had nearly laughed out loud when Landon mentioned the dude ranch.

"A dude ranch? In Alabama? This ain't Montana, Landon. Who do you think is gonna pay money to visit a dude ranch here? And what would they *do* on the ranch? We don't exactly move a lot of cattle from one ranch to another. Those places that do that kind of thing are usually sporting thousands of livestock. Your place has what, three or four hundred?"

Landon had given him three-fourths of the money he'd saved to pay on the past-due notes, and Andy still didn't look impressed.

"I'm sorry. I worked with your grandfather and your father," the older man said. "And I know how important that land is to you and your brothers, but the bank has to be paid. It's just business."

"But we do have six months to get things current. That's what you told John, right?"

"That was assuming you had some form of a business plan in order that'd show us how you aimed to get caught up in six months. The debt just keeps growing, and we can't wait on a pipe dream. I'm sorry, son."

Landon hadn't been called "son" since his father had passed, and he didn't appreciate the term coming from the frowning banker, but he held his tongue. "What do you need to have to show we're working toward getting caught up, and how much time do we have to prove it to you?"

"I'd like to see a decent business plan, something worthy of me bringing to the board here, within a month. And don't just have something on paper. You need to show that you boys are actually doing something to turn the farm around, whether that's selling a whole bunch of beef or finding some way to make money off of your land, but something." He tapped his pen on the paper. "Something other than a dude ranch."

Andy's words plagued Landon's thoughts throughout the day. He'd been so excited about John's idea, and now they needed something else. And Landon had no suggestions. It was too late to plant crops. The beef prices were at a record low. He was not going to section off the land and sell parcels. That's what a lot of the local farmers had done over the years when they hit rough times, and the next thing they knew, an entire little subdivision had sprouted up in the middle of their property. He couldn't let that happen to his daddy's land. He wouldn't.

But he needed a plan. And he needed it within a month.

He'd hoped by the time he finished the day's deliveries—and before he saw his brother—he'd have come up with another idea. But Mr. Ramer only had about an hour's worth of deliveries, and Landon made it home by early afternoon. So when he saw John, he had no choice but to tell him their dilemma.

John walked out of the house and started toward

the barn when Landon climbed out of the truck. "Hey," he said, "might as well come on out and help me with the animals while you're already dirty." He grinned broadly, obviously happy with the outcome of his day. Landon wished he felt the same. "How'd the meeting with Andy go? Everything set?" John asked, still walking toward the barn and not yet realizing that Landon wasn't as enthusiastic about his day.

"Not exactly." Landon joined him and didn't see any reason to sugarcoat his meeting with the banker. "Listen, Andy isn't going for the dude ranch idea."

John's steps slowed. "But we have six months to show them how it can work, right? See, I found this forum through the business center at the college, and I've already talked with a woman from Chicago who thinks she can come down and help us get it started, make sure we have everything set up right from the get-go, on the business end and all. She really seems to know her stuff. I, well, I kind of already asked her about coming down and getting us on track."

"You may want to take back that invitation, I'm afraid. And we don't exactly have six months. We have six months to put the business plan in action, but the bank wants to see the plan within four

weeks, and they want to see proof that we're acting on whatever that plan may be."

"But not a dude ranch."

"Sorry, John. Andy said he couldn't see a dude
ranch flying in Alabama, and he wasn't willing
to budge."

John shook his head. "I'm sure it'll work. And
I think this woman, Dana Brooks, is the one to
help us make it happen."

"It may have worked, but that isn't the plan
we're going to be able to sell the bank right now.
We have to come up with something else, and I've
got to tell you that I've tried to think of something
all day. I haven't got anything."

"Too late for crops. Beef prices are pathetic,"
John said, following the same line of thinking
Landon had. "What are we going to do?"

"I don't know, but we have four weeks to figure
that out. And we're supposed to have a business
plan on paper too. Think you can pull that off in
your first four weeks of business classes?"

John smiled, and Landon had an appreciation
for the fact that his younger brother had always
enjoyed a challenge. "I reckon I will. But it'll help
when we have an idea what that business is going
to be."

Landon grinned, feeling a little better just
knowing that he had some help in the endeavor.

"I'll keep thinking on it, and you do the same. We *aren't* going to lose the farm."

Georgiana sat in the front-porch rocker, leaned her head back and let the memory of yesterday afternoon in the barn consume her thoughts. Not the fear she experienced when she realized someone was in the barn or even the outright panic of knowing a poisonous snake had her in his sights, but the memory of what happened after.

Georgiana, can I hold you?

She'd been so afraid, and Landon's words were so tender, his touch so comforting. He'd used her full name, and there had been something precious about that too. She hadn't cared that they were both "filthy," as her mother had noted upon coming in. The only thing that mattered was that Landon was there, that he cared and wanted to hold her until her fear subsided.

How long had it been since she'd been held like that?

"Georgiana, Abi and I will be leaving in about an hour. Are you sure you don't want to come with us for her school placement test? You've finished your transcriptions for today, haven't you?"

Georgiana nodded, continued moving back and forth in the rocker. She *wanted* to go with Abi, but practically every teacher at Claremont Elementary had known Georgiana when she could see. They would all be staring at her, or become eerily quiet when she entered a room, or try to determine how to get out of her way without making noise. Since she didn't know the layout of the school well enough, she'd need her white cane, and she hated using the cane in front of Abi.

That thing only draws more attention to you.

Pete's voice echoed through her thoughts, and she knew he was right.

"Mom, I don't want to go to the school today. I promised Abi I'd go to her recital, and I will. But that's the next time I plan to get out in public. Going to the square the other night was horrible. People were staring." Her mother inhaled, but Georgiana continued before she could disagree. "I may not be able to see them, but I can feel them."

The rocker next to hers creaked as her mother sat beside her on the porch.

"I had a wonderful time with Abi yesterday at the pond, without the pressure of people staring and whispering. I want to share more time with her like that first and build up to going out, if that's okay."

"Of course it is, and I wasn't going to ask you again," her mother said. "But I do want to talk to you about something else."

"Pete or Landon?"

"Oh, dear, am I that predictable?"

Georgiana reached out, found her mother's hand then squeezed. "It's okay. I know it's only because you care."

"I do," Eden said, "and I'm tired of talking about Pete."

"Me too," Georgiana said with a smile. "So we're talking about Landon."

Her mother laughed softly. "Yes, I guess we are. You were thinking about it, weren't you? While you were sitting out here? About his idea to help you ride Fallon again?"

She'd been thinking about him, but not necessarily the idea that her mother tossed out last night. She'd been thinking of how good it felt to be held by him. And she'd also been thinking about the lie she told him Saturday. How would she ever tell him the truth?

"It'd be good for you to ride again, Georgiana," her mother continued. "And I honestly believe it'd be good for you to let Landon help."

Georgiana pushed her other thoughts aside and concentrated on the subject at hand. No doubt riding Fallon again would make her happy, if it were possible, but she didn't know if she necessarily needed Landon to help her accomplish the task. There were risks involved with spending time with Landon Cutter that didn't involve getting injured riding.

The main risk, as Georgiana saw it, was losing her heart. And if she did, how could she stand being hurt again when he, like Pete, couldn't handle the burden of dealing with her blindness? Or, even more likely, he couldn't forgive himself if he found out what caused it. "I do want to ride Fallon again." She shifted in the seat so that she faced her mother. "But I don't understand why *you* can't help me. It wouldn't be that different than any other riding lesson. And it's like you said, it isn't as though I don't know how to ride. I simply have to remember and apply my old knowledge to doing it without sight."

Her mother huffed out a breath. "Georgiana, I'm fairly certain you realize he doesn't merely want to help you ride again. That young man cares about you. Don't you think he can see that you aren't living anymore, cooped up in this house day in and day out? Yes, he wants to teach you to ride, but he wants more than that, and I think you know it. He wants his old friend back."

Georgiana swallowed, rocked back and forth. "I'm not certain we can be friends like that again." Her heart was already leaning way beyond friendship. She'd hardly been able to concentrate on her transcription at all today because she kept tuning out the doctors and hearing Landon. *Georgiana, can I hold you?* Goose bumps trickled down her arms, an obvious response to the effects his words had on her vulnerable heart.

"Why couldn't you be friends?"

"Too much has changed." She thought of all the possibilities for getting hurt if she let herself get close to Landon again. And for hurting him. "He has no idea what my limitations are now and how difficult it would be to hang around me the way he used to. He doesn't realize how much of a burden it is to try to help someone who is blind."

"Heavens, Georgiana. Every man out there is not like Pete Watson, ready to turn tail and run if a relationship doesn't come easy."

"You didn't say anything about a *relationship* with Landon. You said friendship," Georgiana quickly clarified. "Mom, if you've got your hopes up for something more, then you need to push those thoughts aside."

"And why should I do that?"

"Because I wouldn't even consider it." Georgiana's words grew choppy from the emotion seeping its way in and from the fact that her heart was already trying to consider that very thing. "I couldn't do that to Landon, try to convince him that there could be more for the two of us, be-

cause I would never want him to settle for someone like me."

"If you ask me, he wouldn't be settling, not in
his opinion, anyway. And something else. I may
not be the only one who has their hopes up that
you two will not only rekindle your friendship but
also see if there's more than friendship in the picture." She blew out an exasperated breath. "There,
I said it."

"Mom, please. Don't go there. I do not have my
hopes up for that."

"I'm not talking about you," Eden said. "I'm
talking about him."

"I can't talk about this now," Georgiana whispered, but her heart was already thumping a po-
tentially happy tune. What if Landon did want
something more?

*I'm sorry, Georgiana. I need someone who is
still young. You act like an old woman, sitting in
this apartment all the time and afraid to go out.
I want to live. I deserve to live. I mean, what guy
would want to deal with this all the time?*

Pete's words echoed in her heart, and Georgiana found herself tamping down on the glimmer
of hope.

"If you don't want to talk about Landon's feelings toward you, at least talk about the possibility of accepting his friendship again. You need a

friend, Georgiana, someone to help you gain the courage to get out of this house and live again. And he wants to do that. Start by spending time with him and learning to ride Fallon again."

"Mom, I don't think that's a good idea."

"You were always so happy when you rode. I want to see you that happy again. And I'm sure Abi would love to see you happy." She cleared her throat. "There are only a couple of weeks left until the recital. You need to think about that and start preparing yourself to go back out in the real world again."

"You think learning to ride Fallon will help me with that?" Georgiana knew her mother meant well, but spending that much time with Landon? He'd made her so nervous Saturday that she'd fallen all over herself trying to get away. Then yesterday he'd made her *something*. Excited, nervous and hopeful. And hope had often brutally hurt her in the past.

"I don't know that learning to ride again will do the trick, but I'm certain that spending time with Landon won't hurt. *I'm* not going to teach you to ride again," she said emphatically. "He is."

"What if I don't let him?"

"Then I guess you'll keep sitting in this house, moping away the days and never getting out of your comfort zone. And I will personally raise your daughter, and you'll become an old spinster, destined to sit in one of these rocking chairs until you die."

Georgiana couldn't hold back her smile. "You're terrible."

Eden's rocker scraped on the porch as she scooted closer to her daughter. Then Georgiana felt the warmth of her mother's arm draping around her in a hug. "Honey, I'm only trying to help you. And I can't imagine anything that would help you more than letting a young man who cares about you help you do something that we both know you want to do."

"You really think I could ride again? Without getting hurt?" Have mercy, she couldn't control the hope in her tone.

So you'll try to ride a horse, fall off and kill yourself—or give yourself yet another disability. That's real smart, Georgiana. Leaving Abi with no mother at all. Or even less of a real one.

Georgiana shook Pete's words away and focused on listening to her mother instead.

"That young man killed a snake for you yesterday. Do you honestly think he'd let you get hurt on a horse? Plus, everything I've read on the subject says there's no reason that you shouldn't ride again. You were always a talented rider, very careful too. And Fallon's the most genteel horse around. I've told my riding students that if they want her to stop, they only need to hold their breath. And if they do, Fallon's so good, she stops."

Georgiana smiled. She did have an amazing horse, and Fallon would undoubtedly take extra care if she had Georgiana in her saddle. "Fallon is special, isn't she?"

"She is," Eden agreed. "And so are you, honey. You want to ride her again, don't you?"

Georgiana couldn't lie. "I do."

"And Landon wants to help you," Eden said. Then the front door opened and Abi's fast steps crossed the porch.

"Almost time, Grandma?"

"Yes dear, it's almost time," Eden said. "We'll leave in a few minutes. Why don't you get my purse for me before we go?"

"Okay." Abi's steps moved closer to the rockers. "Love you, Mommy." She hugged Georgiana and kissed her cheek.

"Love you right back."

Abi's steps faded away as she went inside, and Eden didn't wait before broaching the subject of Landon again. "Let him help you, Georgiana." She squeezed Georgiana's arm. "I've been praying for God to give you the help you need to get past all of this, and I think that's what He has done... with Landon."

Georgiana cleared her throat. "Mom, I don't think it'll be that easy."

"Try to focus on something other than all of the negative things Pete said to you over the years. I know he hurt you terribly, but I don't want that hurt to control your life forever. And I can't help but think that there's another young man who would have never turned his back on you. Maybe *he's* the one who will help you learn to trust again, maybe even help you learn to love again."

"Mom, you and I both know that can't happen. I can't let him—" Georgiana started, but Eden interrupted.

"I'll repeat what he told me at church. You are too young and way too beautiful to stop living."

"Landon said that?"

"He did. And he wants to be your friend again, the way you were such good friends back in high school."

"Become friends again," Georgiana repeated, her mind churning that idea. She *had* missed having a true friend. Linda had been terrific to have close by in Tampa, but their friendship was based more on similar circumstances than years of building trust. Georgiana and Landon had known each other so well that she could tell what he was thinking by merely looking into those amber eyes.

She swallowed. She couldn't look into his eyes. That wouldn't be the way she'd be able to tell what he thought anymore. In fact, growing close to Landon again wouldn't be easy without her sight, but she yearned to be close to someone special. And deep in her heart, she wanted that person to be Landon. But how could she get close to him without telling him the truth?

"Give him a chance to be your friend again," Eden coaxed. "If you do that first, then the riding shouldn't be nearly as difficult."

Georgiana's cell phone rang before she could respond. She pulled it out of her jeans pocket and flipped it open. "Hello."

"Georgie, it's Landon."

Her pulse sped up as she immediately recalled his strong heartbeat pulsing against her ear when he'd held her. And she recalled with utter clarity that she wanted to be in his arms again. She inhaled, let it out and focused on keeping her voice steady. "Hi, Landon."

She heard her mother lean against the porch railing while obviously listening to Georgiana's end of the conversation.

"I got your cell number from your mother at church Sunday. I hope it's okay for me to call, because I wanted to ask you about something." He paused. "Did your mom tell you what we talked about?"

"About me riding again?"

"That, and letting me help you do it," he said.

"Yes, she did."

"And?"

Georgiana thought about what would be involved with riding Fallon. There was no way Landon could teach her verbally. He'd be helping her saddle Fallon, helping her mount, helping her in several ways that put him in close proximity. What if that close proximity caused her to feel even more than what she was already starting to feel? Right now, she felt comfort in his arms. She felt safe. But what if she actually felt *desire* stir inside of her again? She hadn't felt that in years, mainly because she'd known that her desire for Pete wasn't reciprocated. But what if her mother was right and Landon might actually still have *those* types of feelings toward Georgiana?

Then she wouldn't be able to let this happen, because she wouldn't want him to become as discouraged with her as Pete had been, once he realized just how limited she was. And how long would it take him to put two and two together and figure out what really caused her blindness?

"I don't know," she whispered.

"Georgie, you can't keep on the way you're living. You need to learn how to enjoy life again, the way you did yesterday on that walk to the pond. And you need to remember how good it feels to have a friend again." He paused. "You need to remember how good it feels for *us* to be friends."

"Be friends again," she said, mulling over his words and the possibilities of his proposition.

"Yeah, friends again," he said, and she could hear the hope in his voice. "Come on, Georgie."

When she didn't readily answer, he continued, "I've finished what I had to do at work and around town today and am almost done with everything around the farm. I'd like to come over and visit with you, tell you what all has been going on in my life. And I'd like for you to do the same. Basically, I'm asking if you want to hang out the way we used to."

"You aren't planning to try to teach me to ride Fallon?"

"I am, but not today."

An afternoon with an old friend visiting and catching up, the way they used to do each day after school. An old friend who protected her, made her feel safe. "Okay," she said, and was surprised that she felt the beginnings of anticipation.

"I'll be there in about an hour," he said, and she could literally hear his smile. "And Georgie?"

"Yes?"

"Thanks."

Chapter Nine

Landon hung up the phone and glanced down at his shirt, stuck to him completely with sweat. His hair was also drenched, and he probably smelled like the inside of the barn. Even though this was the "look" he had yesterday, it wasn't exactly what he was going for when he went to see Georgie today. He'd waited until he was done with his deliveries and his work on the farm with John before he called, but he should've thought to have taken a shower before picking up the phone, in case she said yes.

And she had said yes.

"How about that, Sam? She said yes. Well, she said okay, but that's close enough."

"So, I'm in the next stall, and you're talking to Sam. Makes me feel real special," John drawled.

"Sam doesn't talk back," he said, and left the barn to the sound of John's laughter. He hustled across the yard and took the porch steps two at a time in his eagerness to get ready.

His day had started out rough with that meeting at the bank but maybe, just maybe, it'd end on a much better note...with Georgiana.

After a quick shower, he returned to the barn wearing a denim shirt, jeans, boots and his Stetson. He winked at Sam while he saddled her up. "I know she can't see me but that doesn't mean I should skimp on any of the details." Thankfully, John had headed to the house, so he didn't get any smart remarks from his brother about his conversation with his horse.

Within minutes, he left the barn and made his way toward the mountain. Crisp pine and warm earth mingled to tease his senses as he navigated the trail. He'd missed the stunning girl that had so often shared this scene with him growing up. But today he'd spend time with her, the way they used to, and he couldn't wait.

It'd always been Georgiana in Landon's world. No matter that he was on another continent. No matter if he was in the heat of battle. Even when he suffered from a gunshot wound, he'd thought of Georgiana before anyone else. True, he'd thought a chance to love her was gone, but he'd still missed the girl he'd cared for. And now, there *was* a chance at forever again with Georgiana.

By the time he crested the ridge, his heart thundered so wildly he was certain it pumped against his ribs. He'd been nervous in Afghanistan. Always ready, but always nervous. But this was a different kind of nervous. This was what he'd equate to first-date jitters. Or first day of school. Or meeting a girl's parents. Landon hadn't felt *that* kind of nervous in a decade…until now.

God, help me say the right thing, do the right thing. Don't let me scare her away again.

The moment he finished his prayer, he saw her.

Sunlight captured the red-gold of her hair from where she sat on the log cabin's porch. Ceiling fans whirred full blast across the porch, and the breeze they created caused her long curls to move slightly as she rocked. Landon could tell the minute she heard Sam's gait; the rocker paused briefly and her head turned toward the sound.

"Georgie, it's me," he said softly, while he tied Sam to the hitching post.

"I know," she said. "I heard Sam."

Sam nickered at the mention of her name, and Landon gave her a gentle pat before he left her and moved to the porch. He didn't hurtle up the steps like he had his own earlier. On the contrary, he moved slowly, cautiously, not wanting to scare Georgiana again. He felt as though he were trying to corral a wild mustang…or preparing to take on an abandoned minefield in Afghanistan.

"Okay if I sit with you so we can chat?" Sure, it felt awkward asking her permission to talk, but after what had happened in the barn Saturday, he wasn't taking any chances, even if they had made progress yesterday with that hug.

"Yes, that's fine," she said, but her voice quivered like it did the other day, and Landon hated that she was so apprehensive around him.

He sat in the rocker beside hers but didn't rush into conversation. Instead he simply enjoyed being here again with Georgiana. At his home, he was too busy concerning himself with everything that needed to be done around the farm to sit back and enjoy the ambiance. Here, however, with Georgiana by his side, he enjoyed the serene setting and took pleasure in seeing how well she blended with her surroundings.

"It's a nice afternoon," she said. "Cool for August, I think. But maybe I've gotten used to Tampa."

"It is cooler than usual. Then again, maybe I've gotten used to…other countries."

She nodded, a hint of a smile playing with the corners of her mouth. "Maybe so."

Small talk. Not what he wanted. He had it all ironed out, word for word, everything he wanted to say to Georgiana. But now that he sat beside her with her sweet apple scent teasing his senses, all words escaped him. He didn't have the foggiest inclination of what he'd planned to say to initiate the conversation. But he didn't have to, because Georgiana had already decided how she wanted to start.

"Landon, I know you want to be close again, the way we used to be. But I'm not sure I can. The thing is, I don't find it easy to trust anymore." She shrugged. "I honestly don't know if I can let anyone be close to me again, even if it's you."

He could see the fear overshadowing her petite features. Her eyes were pinched closed and her mouth drawn tight as she waited to see what he would say.

Dear God, let me get this right.

"Georgie, I know Pete hurt you, turning his back on you when you needed him most. But I believe you can trust again." Landon remembered Pete chasing after Georgiana in high school, convincing her that he had changed and that he loved her, that he would love her for life. The thought of him leaving her blind and with a child made Landon's fist curl, and he prayed for the strength not to say exactly what he thought of his old teammate. "I honestly believe you can live again, go out and have fun, be a part of Abi's life, involved in all of her activities, like you were yesterday at the pond. She'll want her momma there for the important things, and I know you want to be there." He remembered how Georgiana had always talked about being a hands-on mom one day. Now was her chance. "But being a part of her life means getting away from the farm. You can't stay in this cabin forever."

"I know that. I mean, I know that Abi wants me to be more than someone she sees at home. And I want to get out more. But just because I *want* to, that doesn't mean I can. I've tried."

He thought of how uncomfortable she'd looked Friday night at the square. He'd seen something similar in soldiers who'd been injured in battle, the fear of what others would think, of what others would do, if they weren't "whole" by the world's standards. They needed encouragement. They needed real friends, people who assured them they were loved. "Let me help you, Georgie. Because I believe I can, and I want the chance to try."

"It won't be easy for me," she whispered, almost as though she were talking more to herself than to Landon.

He had to get her to understand that she didn't have to fear him. Unlike Pete, he would never hurt her or look down on her because of her blindness. "I know it won't, but you won't be on your own. You'll have me to help you."

She took a deep breath. "I think you should understand that this may be more than you bargained for."

He wanted to reach for her, hold her again, but he knew that wasn't what he should do. He needed to take this slow. So he did his best to explain why he wouldn't give up on her. "Georgie, I've seen a lot over the last few years. Some of it good, most of it not so good. And I've dealt with a lot of things that were definitely more than I bargained for." He looked at her, saw the emotions playing across her face, the fear still barely hidden beneath the surface. But this time, he saw something else too. He saw...*hope.*

She fidgeted in the rocker. "You should know that what happened Saturday in the barn wasn't out of the ordinary for me. I freak out over things that shouldn't bother me. It's tough when you feel like you're never totally in control. I trip on a daily basis. I fall down. I jerk away when I'm touched. Honestly, I embarrass everyone around me."

No, she embarrassed Pete, but Landon didn't say that now. Instead, he said, "I can see how someone touching you when you aren't expecting it could be frightening. I wasn't thinking about that Saturday, but I'll be aware of it now. That wasn't your fault. It was mine." He cleared his throat. "You told me you'd give me another chance, hang out with me today and let us work on the friendship that we've put on hold for the past eight years. Still willing to give it a chance?"

She turned to face him, and he saw that her eyes glistened with unshed tears. "I've only had one real friend since I left Claremont, another blind woman I met in Tampa, and now we live in two different states. We talk on the phone, but that isn't the same as having someone around all the time. But if I'm going to be extremely truthful, I would like to have a friend again." She moistened her lips. "And I've really missed our friendship."

"I've missed it too." A major understatement. His life had never been the same since the day Georgiana had left him in that church.

She moved her head in a subtle nod. "Okay. Then, do you have an idea for us to get back on track?"

"I think the best way to fill the gap from then and now is to talk about what happened in between." He desperately wanted to know what had happened to her over those years. How did she react at first when she lost her sight? How did Pete act back then? And what went wrong with their marriage initially? Landon wanted the answers to all of those questions, but from the look on her face, he wasn't sure she was ready or willing to share. Therefore, it was up to him to get the ball rolling. "I was in the army," he said.

She lifted a brow. "Seriously, Landon. That's fairly vague, don't you think?"

"You want to hear about everything?" He knew she did, but he wanted her to realize that he wanted to hear about everything too.

"Yes, I do."

"And are you going to tell me about everything that I missed in your life?"

Fallon whinnied from the barn, and Georgiana leaned her head in that direction. "Fallon wants her afternoon snack." She stood from the rocker. "Do you want to go with me to the barn?"

Landon didn't miss her avoidance of the question, but decided to bide his time. "Sure." He stood and moved down the steps, then watched her do the same.

He was careful not to reach for her as she made her way down. Getting accustomed to Georgie being blind would take time, but he would learn what to do and what not to do. He wanted to be a part of her world again and was willing to take the time and effort to make that happen; however, it was difficult to merely watch her without helping her down the wooden steps. His natural instinct was to reach for her, hold her hand, guide her—but he needed to control those natural instincts until he knew what she was comfortable with and whether she wanted his help.

"I do this all the time," she said, as though knowing he studied her every move, anticipating a stumble or fall. "Don't worry."

"Difficult, but I'll try not to," he admitted. "And I noticed you never promised to reciprocate in the sharing game."

She kept walking toward the barn, but her paced slowed. "Landon, back in high school I told you everything. Every thought, every feeling, every tiny detail about what was going on in my life. Even though I had my friend Linda in Tampa, we were never as close as you and I were before. And I'm not sure I can open up to anyone that much again, because I guess I'm afraid of being hurt again. All I can promise you is…I'll try." She sighed. "Is that good enough?"

"That's good enough." And all he could ask for.

"Okay."

Fallon nickered, growing impatient.

"We should probably go give Fallon what she wants," she said, entering the barn and deftly moving to the burlap sack. "She still likes the Granny Smith apples best."

"I know. I gave her one yesterday while you and Abi were at the pond."

Georgiana withdrew two medium-size apples and then walked to Fallon's stall. "Oh, so you sweet-talked Landon into giving you an extra snack yesterday," she said.

"Yeah, she did." He watched her easily move around the barn. "You already know your way around here well, don't you?" That would help when he started teaching her to ride independently.

Georgiana held out her palm for Fallon to gobble up the treat and patted the mare's nose while she noisily finished off the first apple. "This is where I grew up, and Mom hasn't changed all that much around here since I left. Plus a lot of it has to do with memory and repetition. There are plenty of things you could do with your eyes closed if you tried."

Landon remembered foxholes in the pitch black of night with only the fires from distant bombs providing any means of sight. He'd truly felt blind then, and yet he knew what he had to do and how to do it. "I'm sure you're right."

As if she'd followed his train of thought, she said, "Tell me about the army, Landon. Where were you stationed? What did you do exactly? And I guess what I want to know most of all, were you scared? You said you got shot. How did that happen, and who helped you then?"

He saw a glimmer of the chatty Georgiana he'd known before, and the vision warmed his heart.

Slowly but surely, *his* Georgie was returning. "That's an awful lot of questions to cover at once."

She gave him a soft smile. "We can take them one at a time, and we don't have to cover them all today. But I think you were right. I'll need to learn what's happened to you during the time we've been apart if we're going to rebuild our friendship." She held the second apple out for Fallon. "Plus I admire you for serving our country, and I want to know more about it."

Several of Landon's friends he'd seen around town had said they were glad to have him back. Some had thanked him for his service, but no one asked for details. He assumed eventually John would want to know more about the ins and outs of battle, but the two of them had been so involved in getting Casey off to school and taking care of the farm that they hadn't really had a chance to have the discussion.

The truth was that details of war were intense, private and personal to each soldier. Many didn't want to talk about it at all when they returned to the States. A few would go the total opposite direction and talk about it nonstop, unable to separate the world of war from the world of peace. Landon hadn't had anyone to talk to so far, and somehow the fact that he would share his experience for the first time with Georgiana seemed very right.

"What do you want to know first?" he asked, as Fallon realized she'd finished all of the treats and returned to her paddock.

Georgiana shifted to lean against the stall, pushed a long curl behind her ear and asked, "What *were* you in the army?"

Landon watched the way her fingers moved against the strawberry lock and found himself wanting to know if her hair was as soft and silky as it appeared. Would the curls twine around his finger if *he* pushed that lock away? Yesterday he'd held her close, but he had only thought of comforting her and hadn't really considered the way her hair felt against his palm. Then again, it had been fairly saturated with mud and grass. He smiled at the image, and then realized he hadn't answered her question. "What *was* I?" he asked.

"Like the position or rank." She shrugged. "Whatever you call it. I guess I'm wondering what exactly you did."

Landon thought of the progression of jobs and duties he'd achieved over the years and decided to list them from the beginning. "I guess you could say I followed the typical hierarchy in the army. Started out as a private and worked my way up the ranks to sergeant first class. I was platoon sergeant for 2nd Platoon, Bravo Company, 2nd Battalion of the 505th Parachute Infantry Regiment, which is the 3rd Brigade of the 82nd Airborne Division. I was a jumpmaster," he added, rattling off his unit and information like he always had, because it was second nature to say it with pride, then he saw her brows lift and chuckled. "I'm sorry. That doesn't tell you a whole lot, but I was rather proud of it."

"You should be," she said. "It's amazing how you've given your all for our freedom. I want you to know that. And I hope that people have told you how much they appreciate what all you've done for this country."

He'd heard a few thank-yous over the years, but often people merely smiled at him and looked a little uncertain about what to say. That was all right too, though. The smile said they were thankful, and that was enough. "Some have told me." But none of them had meant as much as hearing it from Georgiana.

"Were you stationed the same place the whole time you were gone, or how does that work? Where all have you been?"

"I started out at Fort Benning, Georgia, for basic training. Then I was stationed at Fort Bragg, North Carolina, for three years, then Vicenza, Italy, for three years and then back to Fort Bragg."

"But you fought in Afghanistan, right?"

Landon glanced at the tattoo on the inside of his left wrist, instantly remembered the sounds of gunfire, bombs and screams. "Yes, I was deployed for three years."

Her mouth flattened, eyes tensed. "It was hard, wasn't it? Hard on your heart?"

He'd never admitted that to anyone. He swallowed thickly. "More than I can explain."

"Oh, Landon," she whispered, and for a moment he thought she might move closer to him, reach to hug him. He yearned for that hug, but she remained still. "I'm so sorry."

He'd never regretted a moment of the time he'd served. "It's part of duty."

"I know, but still, it had to be tough." She ran her teeth over her lower lip. "You want to walk back to the porch?"

"Sure."

He walked alongside her but let her lead and was taken aback once more with how capable she moved without sight. She was a petite woman, no more than five-foot-four to his six-one, even more obvious by the way her long hair covered her entire back and swayed at her waist as she moved. Climbing the porch steps, she easily found her way to the same rocker as before. "I like it out here."

He sat beside her in the next rocker. "I know. It's beautiful. If there was one thing I really missed when I was overseas, it was this view." He immediately realized what he'd done. She couldn't see the scene at all. "I'm sorry, Georgie."

"Don't be. I *know* it's beautiful. I think about that all the time, about everything surrounding me right now. And I'm lucky, because I remember it. Those who've been blind since birth don't have those memories. I'm—I'm very blessed."

"Still, I should have thought before saying that."

"Tell me something." She lifted a hand and pointed toward the end of the porch. "The crepe myrtles at the end of the house. The ones that reach up high enough to fill the window outside my bedroom. Are they blooming now?"

He looked at the tall trees. "They're in full bloom."

She smiled. "I thought so. I have things that I think of specifically to determine certain colors. That was Linda's idea, a way for me to keep my knowledge of the hues. And when I think of pink, I think of those crepe myrtle blooms."

Landon looked at the bright pink flumes tipping each branch of the towering tree. "That's a great reference for pink."

"That's what Linda said too. She thought of cotton candy for her memory of pink, but not me. I always thought of those crepe myrtle blooms and how much I enjoyed looking at them each summer and fall through my bedroom window."

"So Linda wasn't born blind?"

"No, we had that in common. But she'd been blind three years when we met, and she taught me little tips and tricks for helping me cope." She smiled. "She's a great friend."

"I'm glad you had her." She should have had a husband's support, but since she hadn't, Landon was certainly thankful for her friend.

"I don't know what I'd have done without her help." Her mouth crooked to the side. "Mom offered to move me back to Claremont years ago, but Pete and I were going through marriage counseling, so I wanted to stay. And then eventually Linda met her new husband and moved to Miami. Basically, without her in Tampa, I didn't really have a reason to stay."

"I'm glad you had someone to help you out through the rough time."

"I am too."

Landon should have left it at that. He knew he should, but he simply couldn't hold back his thoughts. "Pete should have helped you too, Georgie. Why didn't he?"

She stood quickly, took a step toward the door. Landon saw her move and attempted to scoot out of her way, but he couldn't get his long legs back quick enough, and she stumbled over his boot.

Reflexes taking over, he reached for her, his arms cradling her back as she started to fall.

She didn't jerk away. In fact, in Landon's opinion, she relaxed in his embrace, and he caught himself inhaling deeper to truly experience the apple scent, the warmth of her flesh against his arms. "Are you okay?" he asked, gently easing her upright. "You were falling, and I…reacted."

"Yes," she said, her surprise evident in the single syllable. "Yes, I am okay." And then she smiled. "Very okay, I think."

"That's good."

The sound of a car on the gravel driveway caused him to turn around. "It's your mom and Abi."

"I know. I recognized the sound of her car."

Landon realized that even though she stood fine on her own now, his arms still circled her waist. And he didn't make any effort to move them. Then, as the car grew closer, he reluctantly lowered his arms and put a small distance between them. "I guess I can let you go now."

One corner of Georgiana's mouth lifted. "Probably a good idea. We wouldn't want to get Mom's hopes up too much."

Landon's heartbeat kicked it up a notch. "Her hopes are up for something?"

"Of course," she said. "You know she always liked you."

"I like her too." But not nearly as much as he liked her daughter. He cleared his throat. "I'm going to touch your cheek, if that's okay."

"It's okay," she said, her voice feather soft.

Landon reached out and ran a finger along her cheek, enjoyed the feel of her soft skin as he let it trail along the line of her jaw. "I'll learn what to do, Georgie. I don't want to scare you. And I want to help you."

"You're helping already."

The driveway was long, and Landon was grateful. He took advantage of their last few seconds of privacy, and instead of taking his hand away, he eased his fingertips toward her ear and touched a long red tendril of hair. It *was* silky soft and did indeed curl around his finger. "Beautiful," he said, his voice thick and husky.

Georgiana's lashes lowered, her cheeks instantly flushed. "They're almost here," she whispered.

The car circled the magnolia tree centering the front of the house and then stopped, with Eden and Abi climbing out on opposite sides as Landon moved his hand back to his pocket. "Yeah, they're here," he said.

"Mom, I passed all my tests just fine!" Abi yelled, running toward the porch. "Hey, Mr. Landon," she said. "Can I pet your horse?"

"Sure."

"Can I give her a snack?"

"I bet she'd like that," he said, mesmerized by Georgiana's secret smile. She'd enjoyed his touch. Landon was certain of it.

Abi instantly changed gears and darted toward the barn. "I'll get her an apple."

Eden's knowing smile told Landon that she'd seen at least part of his and Georgiana's exchange. He nodded at the sweet lady, and she took a hand to her heart.

"Abi did great," she said, climbing the stairs. "She has 20/20 vision and her hearing is excellent too."

"That's wonderful." Georgiana moved her hand to the long curl Landon had touched. "Thanks for taking her, Mom."

"My pleasure." She stopped for a moment at the door. "I'm going on in and fixing me a glass of lemonade. I made it this morning, fresh-squeezed. Want me to bring you both a glass?"

"No, I don't think so," Georgiana said.

"No, thank you, Ms. Sanders."

"All righty then." She went in the house.

"I want to spend some one-on-one time with

Abi now, while she's still excited about her placement tests and all. Since I didn't go with her, I at least want to visit with her and find out about everything she did."

He nodded. "I should probably get back to the farm too." Even though he would have stayed here as long as she wanted. No, they hadn't really gotten into a deep conversation about what each of them had done while they'd been apart, but Georgie had made progress. He'd caught her when she was falling, and she hadn't jerked away. Then she'd let him touch her, and today it wasn't due to fear.

Thank You, God.

He'd only scratched the surface of building a new relationship with Georgiana, one that he suspected would be even stronger than before. "Can I come back tomorrow?" he asked. "Would that be okay with you?"

"Yes," she said, and gave him another amazing smile that sent the pretty copper freckles on her cheeks toward those hazel eyes. "Definitely okay with me."

Chapter Ten

❧

"I'm going to touch your cheek, if that's okay."

Georgiana pressed a finger against her face and remembered the way Landon had gently traced her skin. She'd continued to hear his words, feel his touch, ever since he left yesterday. How long had it been since she'd felt so moved? How long had it been since a man had spoken to her with that kind of sweet reverence? From the time she lost her sight, Pete's words had been harsh, degrading, even hateful.

But Landon was nothing like Pete. And she found herself wondering if she might actually be worthy of a man's attention again. Landon had lifted her spirits and made her feel something she hadn't felt in a long time...*wanted*.

She couldn't hold back her smile as she tried on yet another outfit for the tiny audience in her bedroom. "What do you think of this?" she asked her mother and Abi. She'd always had an appreciation for pretty clothes, and being blind hadn't really changed that. However, the fact that she rarely left the farm had caused her to forgo worrying about whether things matched or if her outfit was flattering. But even though she wasn't leaving the farm today, she would have at least one person viewing her choice of clothing. And she wanted to look nice. She turned a full circle then asked, "Is it okay with these shoes?"

"I like those shoes," Abi said.

She'd slipped on some sandals that Pete had given her way back when. Lately she spent most of her day in her barn boots when she was outside or her bare feet when in the house, but she wanted to be prepared in case Landon wanted to go for a walk. Actually, she rather hoped he did. She hadn't had a desire to hike the trails by herself without the ability to see her surroundings, or more specifically when she couldn't see things that might be slithering or crawling nearby, but she did miss the trails, missed that feeling of being completely in the midst of God's creation.

"You sure they match? The shoes, I mean." She remembered that the straps on the Chacos were multicolored but had no idea if the green in the fabric would match the shade of her sleeveless sweater, which Abi had described as "summer-grass green."

Abi giggled. "Yes, Momma. Green is my favorite color on you. But I like your new red dress for my piano recital too. Red is a good color on you too."

"Thanks, sweetie."

"You always look beautiful, Georgiana," her mother added.

"Thanks, Mom." Georgiana had never been one to shop for designer clothing, a trait she'd learned from her mother. They were yard-sale and consignment-store shoppers, not because they were all that limited in funds but because neither of them felt they had to wear something that cost a small fortune or had a particular emblem sewn on the chest to look nice.

Pete hated the fact that Georgiana wasn't a name-brand shopper. When they first moved to Tampa, he'd been adamant that she should blend better with the other wives at his investment firm. But in spite of the fact that Georgiana's clothes were off the discount racks, she thought she blended very well with the other ladies during those company gatherings. Of course, the only picnics and parties she'd attended were at the very beginning of their marriage, before the blindness set in and Pete stopped taking her along for the corporate outings.

She cringed, not wanting to ruin today by thinking back to that time. Too many bad memories.

Instead she wanted to think about potential new memories, potential good memories, with Landon.

"Do you want the matching cardigan?" her mother asked. "The rain this morning left a little chill in the air, and the breeze off the mountain is cool too."

"That's a good idea." Georgiana had been inside working most of the day, but she'd walked to the pond with Abi during lunch and had felt that chill. Skipping stones had quickly become part of their daily routine.

"Want me to get it for you?" her mother asked.

"No, I'll get it." Georgiana knew it was tough for her mom to let her do things herself, but she enjoyed accomplishing tasks, even those as trivial as finding her matching sweater.

She reached into the antique chifforobe that had graced her room since she was a little girl and ran her hands along the edges of the sleeves until she touched satin piping. When she'd first started learning to match clothes blind, she'd had tags sewn in the back of each garment with a Braille description of the color and item. But she never was that great at reading Braille, and she found that practically every item she owned had something about it that made it unique to the touch, like the satin piping on the green cardigan. Before long, she could select her clothes with no problem at all.

"What time is Landon coming over?" her mother asked.

"I'm not sure," Georgiana said. "So I thought I'd go ahead and get ready, just in case. The denim capris look okay?"

"Yes, dear. What are you two planning today?"

"Just talking, finding that friendship again like you suggested. Then maybe, eventually, I'll try riding Fallon again."

"Today?" Abi asked. "You're gonna ride Fallon today? I'm riding Sugar today, and we could ride together! That would be so fun, Mommy!"

Georgiana's heart ached to do that with Abi, particularly because her daughter wanted so desperately to spend more active time with her, yet another reason to try and accomplish this goal. "No, honey, not today, but maybe soon. That's what Mr. Landon wants to help me with."

"Okay," she said, disappointment evident in the single word. "But I really do want to ride with you."

"I want that too." She wanted it so much it hurt.

"Hey Mommy, I like this picture of you on Fallon."

Georgiana heard the frame scoot across the dresser as Abi must have lifted it for a better view.

"Which one is it?"

"The one by the pond with the sun setting in

the distance," her mother said. "You were sixteen, I believe."

"Landon took that picture." Georgiana remembered the very day. "We'd raced back from the ridge, and Fallon and I won." She smiled at the memory. "It was the first time I'd ever won, and he said he wanted to take a picture so I'd remember it, because it'd never happen again."

Abi laughed. "You beat him?"

"One time I did," Georgiana said. "But he was right. It never happened again."

"He was your good friend, huh?" Abi asked, and Georgiana sensed that her daughter still gazed at the photo.

"Yes." A very good friend.

"And now he's your friend again," Abi said.

"Yes." Georgiana smiled. "I think he is."

"It's fun making friends. I made some new friends at my new school yesterday when we did our eye and ear tests. I saw Autumn there. She was in my class at church, and now she's gonna be in my class at school."

"Hannah Taylor's little girl?" Georgiana asked.

"Hannah Graham now," Eden said, "but yes, that's her little girl."

"Her mama was my friend in school too."

"Yeah, Autumn's mommy told me. And she told

me that she misses you there, at church. I was supposed to tell you that."

"That's nice." It'd been years since she graced the door of a church, and even though she still worshipped God in her heart, she missed being with others sharing her faith. But she didn't miss the feeling that everyone stared at her, or hearing people struggle for the right words when they didn't know what to say in conversation.

Would she ever get over that fear? Would she ever be able to attend church with her little girl? If Landon had his way, she would.

I honestly believe you can live again, go out and have fun, be a part of Abi's life, involved in all of her activities. She'll want her momma there for the important things, and I know you want to be there.

His words had touched her heart, but the fact that he believed in her stirred her soul.

God, please, You know how much I want to be a part of Abi's world. And I'd love to really live again, the way Landon described. Help me to find the courage, Lord.

"Autumn said she likes my hair, 'cause it's red. And I told her I liked her hair too, 'cause it's brown."

Georgiana grinned, happy her daughter hadn't had a problem at all with the move to Alabama. Abi adjusted so well to change, even developing a little bit of that Alabama drawl. Then again, that may have been because her life started out with so many changes, beginning with Georgiana and Pete trying to make things work. Then learning to cope with her blindness. And next, she and Abi moving in with Linda while Georgiana and Pete were separated. Thankfully, Abi had loved Linda and seemed to enjoy the three of them living together. She'd even been the flower girl in Linda and Gary's wedding.

That memory reminded Georgiana of the phone conversation she'd had late last night. Pete called and asked that Abi perform the same function in his wedding. And *that* was the way he'd told Georgiana that he was getting married again.

"It wasn't that he didn't want to be married," Georgiana said softly. "He just didn't want to be married to me."

"What, Mommy?"

The color drained from her face. Occasionally, the fact that she couldn't see caused her to forget that she wasn't the only person in a room and should never utter her thoughts aloud. "Nothing, sweetie. I was just thinking."

Georgiana heard her mother's soft sigh and knew that she hadn't missed the comment. As usual, Abi barely paused in her chatting, which kept Georgiana from having to offer any additional explanation.

"Autumn colors real good too," she continued. "At Sunday school, she colored Joseph's coat and stayed in the lines the whole time. I got out of the lines a little, but not too bad. There were a lot of stripes on his coat, so it was kinda hard."

"You did fine," Eden said.

"Yes, I'm sure you did," Georgiana added. Like most kids her age, Abi loved any kind of craft or art. She always brought her projects to Georgiana so she could "see" what she'd made, and Georgiana wished that she had that option. It didn't seem to bother Abi that her momma couldn't do more than touch the artwork, probably because she didn't know any different. In Abi's world, she'd always been blind.

"Your makeup looks pretty," Abi said, interrupting Georgiana's thoughts.

"Does it?" Georgiana asked. "Really?" Makeup was more difficult than matching clothes, and she typically limited it to a little lip gloss, more to keep her lips moist than to actually serve as a beauty accessory. But today she'd found her eye-shadow case and had attempted to put a light brown shadow on her crease and a shimmery taupe on her lid. Or that's what she thought she'd put on, if she picked up the compact that she thought she'd picked up and if the colors were where she believed they were inside the case. She'd never taken time to label her makeup, because she rarely used it. "I didn't put too much?"

"It's very pretty," her mother said, her words holding a good deal of an emotion Georgiana couldn't pinpoint.

"Grandma, can I go on out and see if the other kids are here yet?"

"Sure, honey." Eden had several riding lessons scheduled for this afternoon, and since Abi's age group came on Wednesdays, she'd naturally take a lesson too.

Georgiana listened to her daughter's quick steps exiting the house and the front door slamming. Then she turned toward her mother. "Mom, is something wrong?"

"No, dear," she said. "Nothing's wrong. It's just that I'm glad to see you trying again."

"Trying?"

"To live."

Georgiana again thought of Landon's words and nodded. "Me too."

"I know it's been hard, but it hurts me to see you shut yourself off from life. And this, with Landon, well, I think it's exactly what you need. You look happier today than I've seen you in a very long time."

She smiled. "That's because I am."

"See, Landon is already helping you," her mother said. "Just look at that smile."

Georgiana realized she *had* been smiling a lot today. She couldn't help it. She thought about Landon, about all of the beautiful things he'd said to her, and she simply couldn't help but smile.

"Let him in, Georgiana. Give him a chance to get closer to you. Open your heart and talk to him, tell him everything the way you used to. You've kept so much bottled inside, and I know you always felt comfortable talking to Landon. Don't you think it'd do you good to have that kind of relationship with someone again? With him again?"

Georgiana had told Linda pretty much everything she was feeling, so she had told *someone*. But her mother was right; she hadn't talked to anyone who knew her both before and after the accident. "I think it would do me good," she admitted, but she also knew one of the main things Landon would want to know was what caused her blindness. He'd asked once, and she'd given him a vague answer. Or rather, a partial truth. But she knew there was no such thing. A half truth was a lie. And *that's* what she'd given.

"He said he wants me to tell him everything, all about what has happened to me since we've been apart."

"You went through a lot. Losing your sight was

only part of it, and Landon understands that. Talk to him the way you used to. Start with where you left off and go from there."

"Where we left off?"

"That day in the church. You told me what you felt that day, what you realized after he came to see you and the reason your mind was elsewhere when you left the church parking lot and pulled out in front of that truck, but have you ever told Landon?"

"You know I haven't. It took me several years before I even told you. And he left for the army right after I got out of the hospital, so I never got the chance."

"Then that's the perfect place to start. He deserves to know."

"I married Pete, Mom. Telling Landon what I was feeling back then isn't going to change that." Plus, telling him what caused the wreck was only part of the story.

"No, but it might change the way Landon feels about you choosing Pete."

The front door banged again, and then Abi yelled into the house. "Hey, Mommy! Grandma! Mr. Landon is here!"

"No time like the present," Eden said, gently touching Georgiana's hand before she left the bedroom and started down the hall.

Georgiana listened to her mother's footsteps fade. *Dear God, stay with me. I need all the strength I can get, and I know You can provide.* She went downstairs and heard her mother ask Landon about his day and then tell him she was heading to the barn to give riding lessons.

"Hey," he said.

She didn't have to ask if he'd turned his attention to her; she could hear it in his tone. Her heart fluttered in response. "Hey," she replied.

"You look really nice."

Again, she could hear how much he meant the words, and she felt her cheeks heat. "Thanks."

There was an awkward pause, then Landon cleared his throat and asked, "Walk with me?"

Here he was, a guy who'd undoubtedly done amazing things serving the country, but in those three small words, Georgiana heard a hint of fear, as though he was afraid she'd say no. On the contrary, she'd been waiting to see him all day. "Okay. Where to?"

"The ridge, if that's good for you."

Their special place to talk when they were teens. Yes, that was perfect. "That's good for me. Just let me get my cane." Walking without her white cane around the house and barn was one thing, navigating the trails was something else.

"Tell you what, why don't you leave it here and

let me guide you. I mean, if you're going to ride Fallon, you won't be using a cane. You'll use me and Fallon as your guides. Might as well get used to half of that equation."

The other night at the square she'd held her mother's forearm, and that'd worked fine. But holding her mother's arm and holding Landon's were two completely different things. One was a family member who cared about her. And the other was a man, a handsome, thought-provoking man, who also cared about her…and made her insides quiver. She concentrated to slow her racing pulse. "You're sure you wouldn't mind? Like I've told you before, sometimes I trip. And I've been known not only to topple, but to take everyone along for the fall."

He laughed. "Can't imagine anyone else I'd rather fall for."

Georgiana's skin tingled at the dual meaning, but she swallowed past the nervousness. Would he—could he—fall for her? The way he did back then?

"So, you going to let me help?" he asked. "Because if you turn me down, I'll probably pout. I don't take rejection well. At all."

She held out her hand. "Well, I wouldn't want to make a soldier feel rejected."

He took her hand and a rush of warmth shimmied up her arm. Being with a man again—being with Landon again—threw her already heightened senses into overdrive.

"I can actually navigate the steps pretty good on my own," she said, not wanting him to think her completely helpless.

"I know you can. I saw you handle them perfectly fine yesterday, but humor me." He lowered his voice. "The truth is, I really want to hold your hand."

Another shiver of awareness trickled over her, and Georgiana was shocked to realize that she recognized the old feeling. *Desire.*

"Is that okay, Georgie? For me to hold your hand?" His voice was husky, just above a whisper.

She swallowed. He already held it in his grasp, their hands intertwined, finger to finger, palm to palm. And she had the strongest urge to tell him that not only was it okay, but she never wanted him to let go. However, she kept the impulsive reply in check and simply said, "Yes, it's fine."

"Then we're ready to hike," he said as they descended the steps and then walked in front of the porch.

Georgiana heard the children at the barn laughing and chatting as they prepared for their riding lesson and naturally heard her own daughter's voice stand out from the others. "Sounds like Abi is having fun."

"I think she is. She's laughing at something one of the other kids did," he said, "but I bet you heard that, didn't you?"

"Yes, I did." She once again noticed the drastic contrast in the way Landon treated her and the way Pete had treated her. Pete assumed that because she couldn't see, she couldn't determine anything. He never considered the possibility that she could decipher quite a lot merely by hearing.

But Landon obviously did.

They took a few more steps, and she knew they were near the hitching post where he'd tied Sam yesterday, but she didn't hear any sound from Landon's horse. "Did you put Sam in a stall?"

"I didn't ride Sam. I walked."

"It's a nice day for a walk," she said. "So cool and fresh outside with the breeze and all."

"These early-morning showers are giving us a little relief from summer's heat, so I thought we should take advantage of it today with a walk."

"And since I can't ride yet," she said.

"The operative word being *yet*."

He really did believe in her, and his belief was slowly but surely seeping into Georgiana too. *Maybe I will ride again.* "You're still as confident as you were in high school, aren't you?" she asked.

"I try."

Georgiana enjoyed the way he made her feel so at ease. She also enjoyed the freedom of hiking the trails again and paid attention to her footsteps to determine each change in terrain. She knew from past experience that the trail often altered between pine straw, leaves, soft earth and flat rock. The last thing she wanted to do was slip and fall. Scratch that; the last thing she wanted to do was plummet…and take him with her for the ride.

Can't imagine anyone else I'd rather fall for.

His statement filled her thoughts and she smiled.

"Okay," he said.

"Okay, what?"

"Okay, if you're going to smile like that, you're going to have to tell me why."

"I'm just very happy today. Happier than I've been in a long time."

"Georgie, I think I should let you know that I had no idea your marriage hadn't gone well. I had prayed that you would be happy forever and didn't have any reason to think that wasn't the case when I was away, or I would have checked on you. You were my best friend, but I wasn't there when you needed a friend most."

"I told you we shouldn't see each other again. You were just doing what I asked." She remembered the very moment she'd said the words in the hospital. He'd come to see her after the wreck, and she'd asked him to leave *after* telling him she was still marrying Pete.

Landon cleared his throat but didn't comment, and Georgiana didn't blame him. She knew she'd hurt him back then. What was left to say?

Plenty, her mind whispered, *if you tell him the whole story.*

They continued walking, the sounds of the children fading in the distance as they neared the wooded trail. The air turned cooler as they evidently stepped beneath the cascading trees. She focused on keeping her steps steady and held his hand as she moved. Luckily, the path was relatively smooth and easy to navigate. Even so, a loose clump of pine straw caused her shoes to slide. His other hand instantly caught her forearm and helped her stay secure, and Georgiana was overcome by the warmth of him next to her, holding her, protecting her, the same way he had after her near miss with the copperhead.

"You okay?" he asked.

His hands held her steady, and she fought the impulse to melt against him and simply ask him to hold her that way until all her fears were gone. But she managed a smile and eased away from the close contact. "Yes, I'm fine."

"You're doing great."

"Thanks."

He had always been there to help her growing up, not only physically but emotionally as well. It bothered her that she hadn't realized that he'd simply been trying to help her when he'd warned her about her future husband. Because that day in the church hadn't been the first time he'd tried to tell her the truth about Pete; that was simply the first time he'd also told her the truth about how he felt.

Her steps turned easy as they connected with the flat rock of the ridge. "Are we there?"

"Yes," he said. "You want to sit down?"

She nodded. "After I take this sweater off." In spite of the coolness of the afternoon, she was warm from the walk. Or maybe it was the topic of conversation that had a trickle of perspiration slipping down her spine.

His hands moved against her arms as he helped her out of the cardigan, and Georgiana enjoyed each slight contact of his skin against hers. She shivered and knew it wasn't entirely due to the breeze against her arms in the sleeveless tank. Then his fingers tenderly brushed hers as he took the cardigan from her hand.

"I should have brought a blanket," he said. "I'll remember that next time."

"Is the rock muddy? Dirty?" She'd already crouched down to sit on the smooth stone.

"No, but I figured you'd like a blanket, something softer than the hard rock."

She felt his warmth again as he sat beside her, not close enough that they touched but close enough for her to sense his presence, and she turned her face toward his. "We never used a blanket when we sat up here in high school."

"I know, but I thought you might want one now."

"Because I'm older?"

"Nah, because you're a girl, and girls tend to like their creature comforts."

She heard his jeans slide against the rock, and then a small grunt that said he'd repositioned himself. "Are you lying down?"

"Flat on my back and looking up at the sky peeking through the trees, same way I did back when we were in school. Unlike you. You always stayed seated upright because you didn't want to put your hair on the ground."

Georgiana smirked, placed her palms on the rock beside her and then lowered her back to the ground. "I can wash my hair."

His low chuckle easily rolled out, and she heard him move again. "Here, Georgie. Let me put your sweater under your head."

"Still think I'm afraid of a little dirt?" she asked, but she lifted her head enough for him to slide the cardigan underneath, the back of his hand brushing against her neck. "You did see me after my splash in the pond, right?"

He laughed. "That I did, but I'm sure the sweater will make the rock a little more comfortable."

She settled her head against the soft fabric. "It does." Then she relaxed and soaked in the sounds of the woods, birds tweeting, crickets chirping and tree branches shifting in the breeze. The combination created a calm reprieve that she hadn't felt in a very long time. *Peace,* that was the sensation she experienced here...with Landon.

"Thank you," she whispered.

"For?"

"For bringing me here today."

"You're welcome."

They stayed silent for several minutes, then Landon whispered, "You hear that?"

Georgiana had heard a different sound adding to the mix, but had assumed it was leaves falling or a small animal scampering over pine straw. "I hear something," she whispered back. "What is it?"

"Rabbit, a baby rabbit. Not much more than a cotton ball with feet."

She tuned her ear to the distinct sound, thought about the fluffy rabbits she'd raised growing up. Hers were white. More than likely, the one nearby was brown, a typical wild bunny living on the mountain. "Brown?"

"Light brown, and fairly fat for a baby," he said. "We'll need to bring Abi up here sometime so she can see the trail and the animals. Maybe even that bunny." The scampering turned into a rustling, and Landon announced, "We spooked him. He left."

Georgiana wished she could see the tiny bunny, but at least she knew about it through Landon. And he was right; Abi would love to come here. It touched her that he'd naturally thought about her daughter. "Let's bring her tomorrow."

"Supposed to rain, but if it doesn't, that's a date. If it does, we'll make it the next day."

"Does that mean you're coming to visit every day?"

"Nah, just every day until you tell me to stop."

She laughed. "Works for me."

"Good."

Georgiana realized she hadn't followed through with talking to him about what really happened at the church, but she just couldn't do it, not yet. And maybe he'd forgotten about their plan to "share."

She could tell he'd changed his position once more, and assumed that he was on his side, probably looking right at her. The realization made her feel both vulnerable and sensual. She enjoyed this closeness. It'd been a long time since she'd felt so comfortable and at ease with anyone.

"So," he said, "let's catch up on the years we lost." His words were delivered not far from her face. "I want to know what happened during the time we were apart. What was it like for you when the blindness started? And how did things change so much with you and Pete?"

So much for thinking he'd forgotten. She wanted to talk to him about it, but she wasn't ready yet. Besides, she had a lot of things she wanted to know too. And his life had been so much more interesting. "First I have a few questions for you."

"You're stalling."

She couldn't deny the truth. "Do you mind?"

"No, as long as you promise this street will go two ways eventually."

"Okay," she said. Eventually. *God, give me the courage to tell him, and please protect him when he learns the truth. Don't let him blame himself.*

"All right then, it's a deal," he said. "Ask away."

"Okay." She'd been thinking about everything she wanted to know all day, but the main question that kept coming to mind was, "Did you have anyone you were close to over the years we were apart? Someone you could trust and count on and confide in? The way you confided in me back in high school?" She took a breath, then went ahead with the real heart of her curiosity. "I guess I'm asking if, while we were apart, did anyone take my place in your world?"

His words came near her left ear. "Are you asking if I had a girl I was close to, Georgie?" His breath feathered over her cheek with each word, and she sensed her nerve endings straining to get closer to the magnificent sensation. It'd been so long since she'd been alone with a man, and even longer since she'd been alone with a man without fear of embarrassment or ridicule.

But she didn't fear anything now.

"Georgiana, is that what you're asking?" he repeated, and she realized she was so lost in the sensation of him that she'd forgotten to answer.

"Yes," she said breathlessly. "Did you have a girl who was special to you?"

"I met someone in Kuwait and we talked for a while, but there were too many differences. And way too many barriers." His words were delivered even closer to her now, and she caught a hint of mint in his breath.

She swallowed. "Other than her?"

"Other than her, my only close friends were the ones in my unit. I had three guys that were practically brothers to me while we were together. They were the ones I confided in while I was gone, while we were all together."

"Did they know about me?" she asked, and then

wondered if that was too personal a question or if it sounded as though she thought too much of herself. But Landon didn't hesitate in his answer and didn't sound as though he minded her curiosity.

"Yes," he said. "They did."

"What did you tell them? About me, I mean?"

"I told them the truth. That I never got over losing you, Georgie."

She didn't know what to say to that. But the awareness that he'd confided something so personal made her realize that Landon now had vital people in his world that she'd never even met. They'd grown up knowing everything about one another, all about each other's friends and practically everything about what they'd both seen or done during their formative years in Claremont. But now there was a gaping hole in their history, and she wanted to know more about the people who were an important part of his world while she wasn't. "Your three friends. Are they still overseas? Or are they back home too?"

"Neither." He paused, waited a moment more and then added, "They didn't make it back."

Awareness gripped her heart. "All three of them?"

"All three of them," he said. "I have a tattoo on the inside of my left wrist that reminds me of them, and there isn't a day that goes by that I don't look at that tattoo, think about their lives and realize that my name could've easily been inked on someone's wrist as well. We're all so close to death when we're over there. At all times, we're close. We don't think about it, don't really realize it, until we lose a brother in battle."

"I'm so sorry, Landon." Emotion overtook her. Those three *were* brothers to him over there, and now they were gone.

What if something had happened to Landon, and she'd never had a chance to be with him like this again?

He cleared his throat. "It was hard, but I dealt with it."

She wanted so badly to see his tribute to his friends. And she wished she could have been with Landon to help him through the grief. "What is the tattoo? What does it look like, and what does it say?"

"It's a rifle stuck in the ground behind a pair of boots with a helmet on top of the rifle. Dog tags hang from the trigger guard. Mike and John were killed by an improvised explosive device, or what we'd call an IED. Basically a car bomb. Their tattoos state their rank, name, unit, date they were killed and then simply Iraq. Calvin was a former soldier of mine who later went Special Forces. His tattoo has his name and rank, the province in

Afghanistan where he was killed, as well as the Special Forces motto. He was killed in a firefight."

"That had to be horrible, losing all of them." She couldn't even imagine the pain of losing friends that way.

"It was," he said, his anguish evident in his tone. "I was supposed to have been with Mike and John that day, but it was just two days after I got hit in the shoulder, so I wasn't with my unit."

Her heart stilled. "Two days after you were shot, you mean?"

"Yeah."

"So if you hadn't been shot, then you would have been killed in that car bomb," she said, the power of the statement sending chills down her spine. "Is that right?"

"If I hadn't been shot, then yeah, I'd have been with my guys."

Landon could have died, and she wouldn't have had the chance to talk to him again and to tell him how much she cared. She closed her eyes and concentrated.

"Georgie, it was a long time ago, and I've dealt with it."

She said a silent amen then said, "I was praying. Thanking God."

"Thanking Him for what?"

"For letting you get shot."

There was a tiny pause of silence, then Landon's laughter echoed through the trees, rolling out with such force and such abandoned happiness that Georgiana couldn't help but join in. "S-sorry," she said, holding her side. "That didn't come out right."

"It's okay." His laughter filtered through his words. "I'm just thinking that if I'd have been recording you when you said that, I'd probably have a million hits on YouTube."

"Very funny. You know what I meant."

"Yes, I do," he said. "And it's very sweet that you're glad I got shot."

"Landon, that *isn't* what I meant."

"I know. But you have to admit, it's pretty funny. Can't wait to tell John."

"Great," she said. "Now I can look forward to him ragging me whenever I run into him."

"Just like old times."

She nodded, remembering how much fun all of them used to have, the Cutter boys and Georgiana, riding horses, running through the fields, teasing each other nonstop and enjoying a simple life. Before the world intervened with all of the complications and trials it had to offer.

The thought of complications and trials reminded Georgiana of something her mother had told her before Landon returned home, that

John Cutter had been working three jobs and had seemed to be having a tough time on his own raising Casey and running the farm. And Landon was working at the feed store, when she would have thought he'd have come back and merely run the farm, the way his father had done when they were growing up. "Landon?"

"Yeah?"

"Are things okay with your farm?"

He audibly inhaled, then thickly exhaled. "I know you always seemed to be able to read my mind back when we were in school, but what made you ask that? Because I'm trying my best not to think about it, but yeah, there's a lot going on with our farm."

"Just thinking about how things have changed since we used to sit up here and talk, and mom had mentioned John working three jobs, and now you're working at the feed store and trying to run the farm too, right? Is everything okay?"

He cleared his throat. "Not yet, but it will be. We've just got to figure out how."

She could tell he was trying to make it sound better than it was, and if they were working that much and trying to run the farm on their own, things weren't good. "Maybe I can help you figure something out. We used to be pretty good at talking through things together."

He chuckled. "Yeah, but that was typically homework assignments or how to win the homecoming float contest, not quite the magnitude of saving a farm."

Saving the farm? Georgiana frowned. It was worse than she suspected. "What have you got to do?"

"Come up with a business plan, one that shows how we can turn the farm into a profitable business, in a month. And show that we're working toward putting the plan into place." He sighed, then added, "We've got six months to get our debts caught up, or we'll lose the farm."

Her gasp was instant.

"But we aren't going to lose it," he said emphatically. "We just haven't figured out how we're going to keep it yet. John had an idea about starting a dude ranch."

"A dude ranch," Georgiana said, picturing the images of dude ranches she'd seen on television before she lost her sight. They looked like so much fun. "I think that'd be a great idea! I'd never have thought of having one in Alabama."

"Yeah, and I think that's the problem. Andy Cothran said it'd never fly. John feels pretty certain it would, and he's even been talking to some woman from Chicago that he thought could help us get it started."

"I know Andy. He's been at the bank forever, hasn't he?"

"Yeah, and he isn't exactly open to change."

"No chance of convincing him to go with a dude ranch?"

"Not in four weeks," Landon said. "But I suspect John's going to keep pecking at the idea. In the meantime, though, we have to come up with something that we know will make money and put that idea in a business plan for the bank."

"I'll think about it, and I'll talk to mom. Surely with all of us putting our minds to it, we can come up with something."

He touched her cheek, and she didn't jerk away. She hadn't known he was going to touch her, but she felt so secure here, so comfortable beside him, that it hadn't scared her at all.

"Thanks," he said, "for offering to help. And for listening to my troubles. That wasn't exactly what we came up here for."

"Now, I don't know about that. We always talked about our troubles up here."

"I guess we did, didn't we?" He paused then continued, "Georgie, I've told you a lot about what happened to me while I was gone and even what's going on in my life right now. Do you think you could at least tell me a little about what happened with you?"

She'd known this was coming, but even so her nerves were a tangled mess. She took a deep breath, let it out and focused on relaxing against the cool flat rock.

"Still can't talk to me?" he asked.

She shook her head. "It isn't that. I'm trying to figure out where to start." Then she remembered her mother's words. *Start where you left off.* And she knew exactly where they'd left off.

"That day in the church, when you came to see me," she said, "and when I ran away."

"Yeah." His voice had grown husky, and she could tell for certain that he looked directly at her. Odd how she still felt the anxious feeling of knowing a guy was looking at her even when she couldn't see.

She gathered her courage. "I never told you why I left the church the way I did."

"I assumed you were trying to get away from me," he said, "and then that caused your wreck."

She should have known he blamed himself, even if he didn't know everything about the reason she ran. She shook her head. Landon thought she was running from him, when in fact, she'd been running *to* him. "I had to drive, had to think. I thought I would ride around town for a while and then find Mom, talk to her and see what she thought about what I believed I simply *had* to do."

"What you had to do?" he asked. "What did you have to do?"

"Cancel the wedding."

Chapter Eleven

Landon's mind reeled. Georgie had planned to cancel her wedding? Because of him? But that didn't make sense, not with what she told him back then.

"After the accident, when I came to see you in the hospital, you said you never wanted to see me again. You said what happened in the church was a mistake." He knew he had his facts right about her words, because each and every one of them had haunted him over the past eight years.

"I know what I said. And if I could go back and do any time of my life over, believe me, that'd be the time."

"So that *wasn't* the truth? You didn't want me to leave?"

"When I woke in the hospital and realized that I'd had that accident leaving the church, I believed it was God's way of showing me that what I was planning to do was wrong. I was putting myself before everyone else. All of those people who had come to town for the wedding and were in that hospital praying for me, all of the families and friends who were expecting me to marry Pete, and then there was Pete."

"Pete," Landon repeated.

"He hadn't done anything to make me *not* want to marry him. At that time, he'd done nothing but tell me how much he wanted to be my husband and to stay together for life. Grow old together, that's what he said." She shook her head, her strawberry curls shifting against her cardigan. "I couldn't let everyone down. I just couldn't. And I couldn't let Pete down. I'd promised to marry him."

"But you weren't married yet."

"No, and I shouldn't have gone through with it, I know that now. I was having doubts about it even before you got to the church. But I couldn't back out. I couldn't." She turned her face toward the treetops, away from Landon.

"How was he, Georgie? Pete? When the blindness happened, how did he handle it? You said you'd only been married a few months."

She seemed to contemplate what to say. "It was hard for him. He'd expected this perfect marriage," she said, then added, "a perfect wife."

Landon couldn't handle her making excuses for

Pete. "He married you for better or worse, in sickness and in health. Those were the vows he took."

"I couldn't blend with the other wives from his office. He wanted to be involved, be active, participate in things the way a normal newlywed couple would do. But I got pregnant within weeks of the wedding. Then we realized that my blurred vision wasn't something that was temporary, and then it quickly got worse."

"And Pete didn't handle that well," Landon said, remembering his quarterback's love of "perfect" things.

"He didn't see me as desirable anymore," she said, her mouth tightening with the statement as though she were fighting tears.

Landon clenched his jaw. If Pete Watson wasn't a fool, he'd have spent every waking moment reminding her just how desirable she was. "Georgiana, you're beautiful. You've always been beautiful, and you'll always be beautiful. Inside and out."

Her hand moved to her chest, eyes looked so focused on him that he would almost believe she saw him. "You don't need to say that, Landon. I wasn't fishing for a compliment."

"I was only stating the truth." He reached toward her face and tenderly ran a finger along her jaw. She didn't flinch and in fact seemed to turn toward the touch.

"Landon?"

"Yeah?"

"How *do* I look now?" She frowned slightly. "I mean, my mother says I still look like I did in high school, but I wonder if she isn't fudging the truth a little to keep me from getting down. And Abi's like any little girl; she isn't going to say anything negative about her mom. But you know, I often wonder. The doctor said my eyes still look the same, but I can't understand how that could be. And I have all of those girly fears. Am I starting to go gray? Are my freckles darker than before? Is my skin healthy looking, or too pale?" The frown slid up a bit. "I know, I shouldn't care. But I can't help it."

Landon felt like an idiot. She hadn't had anyone to ask about her physical appearance? "Pete never told you how you look?"

"He told me that I looked fine and that I shouldn't worry about it. Kind of the same thing my mom always says. But I do worry about it. I think that's human nature to wonder, don't you?"

"Definitely." He thought of wounded soldiers, particularly those with facial lacerations, asking about the extent of their injuries. Each one wanted to know how he appeared to others, how he would appear to his girlfriend or wife when he returned home; Georgie was no different.

"So, will you tell me?"

He rolled up higher on his side, so he could truly study her features. Then he began to describe every detail of the only woman he'd ever really loved. "Your hair is the same shade as in high school, red with blond intermingled through the curls. A true strawberry blonde if there ever was one."

"Abi's hair is the same color, right?"

"Yes. In fact, she looks just like you did when you were that age."

"That's what Mom says."

"Well, she's right. I remember you back then, and Abi is the spitting image."

"I like knowing that."

He let a soft strawberry curl slide through his fingers. He wanted to tunnel his fingers through the entire length, cradle the back of her head and ease her face closer. But he needed to take his time. Pete had hurt her, and Landon wanted to slowly and steadily show her she was worthy of a man's love, worthy of *his* love.

"Any gray?" she whispered.

He smiled. "There isn't a gray hair to be seen, and your skin is still healthy, not too pale at all."

"That's good. Not that I mind gray hair, but I'm not quite ready for it yet."

Landon grinned. She looked as though she was feeling better about herself already, and he was thrilled to be the cause of the transformation. "Abi's freckles are a lot like yours too, sprinkled across her nose—" he moved a fingertip to the bridge of her nose, then slid it over the adorable sprinkle of freckles on her right cheek "—and then a little lighter on the cheeks."

Her eyes fluttered closed in response.

"Yours are still the same hue as high school," he continued, "a pale copper that only brings more attention to the gold flakes in your eyes."

She opened her eyes, and he saw those specks of gold. Have mercy, she really was beautiful. He hated that she doubted the fact.

"Do my eyes really still look the same, Landon? Tell me the truth."

He looked directly into the hazel depths, and his heart ached that she couldn't return his gaze. "They look the same," he said, but wouldn't lie to her by withholding the obvious, "but different."

"How do you mean?"

"Your eyes are as stunning as ever, Georgie. A marbled brown and green, with tiny bits of gold making them look like you're gazing into the sun at all times." He hesitated, then added, "But it's like they are looking through me, instead of at me."

She nodded, as though already suspecting—or knowing—this trait. "And does that make you feel weird? Does it make me look weird?"

"You know what it feels like to me?"

"No, but tell me, please."

"It feels like of all of the people in the world, you're the only one who looks at me and doesn't see the physical. You see more. You see the soul." He nodded, knowing that was exactly the right way to describe what he felt when those eyes peered at him. "That's exactly how it feels."

"Thank you."

He smiled. "You're welcome."

She ran her teeth across her lower lip, and Landon remembered the gesture well. She wanted to say something.

"What is it, Georgie? What else do you want to know?" he asked, then coaxed, "Come on. You never held back from asking me questions before. If we're going to be that close again, you've got to tell me what you're thinking."

"It's a little embarrassing."

"Try me."

"I've got to admit, I've been wondering more than what I look like."

"Okay, I'm listening."

Her cheeks tinged with pink as she explained, "I've been wondering what *you* look like now, Landon."

He blinked. Not what he was expecting.

"Mom said you still look the same, like Matthew McConaughey," she said with a slight laugh.

"Your mother said that?"

"Well, that was how I always described you in high school," she said. "So she said you still looked the same."

"I never heard you describe me that way." He was floored by the honesty. Landon had thought he and Georgie didn't have any secrets back then, but obviously they had more than he realized. One, he'd never told her he'd fallen for her, not until it was too late. And two, she'd never told him she thought he looked like a movie star. Matthew McConaughey at that.

"All right. Don't go getting all conceited on me. Is your chest swelling?"

"I've gotta admit, yeah, maybe the chest is swelling a little."

"Just never mind," she said, shaking her head as she started to sit up from the rock.

He laughed. "Never mind about what? You tell me you thought I looked like Matthew McConaughey and then you tell me to never mind?

Oh, no, you don't." He tapped her shoulder. "What else were you going to say? I'm all ears."

"It wasn't what I wanted to say," she said, her voice quivering slightly. "It's what I wanted to do."

The nervousness in her tone let him know she wasn't joking. He sobered. "Hey, what is it, Georgie? What do you want to do? I'll help you if I can. You know I will."

"I want to touch your face, to *feel* what you look like now."

His eyes widened. Again, not what he was expecting. But he should have thought about it, the fact that she couldn't see him anymore, and the only way she'd really know if he'd changed over the years was via touch. "I don't know why I didn't think of that," he said, sitting up and then scooting toward her on the rock. "Okay."

"Okay...what?"

"Okay, see—feel—if I've changed."

One corner of her mouth lifted, and she made no move to reach for him. "Great," she said.

"What?"

"Now I'm too embarrassed that I asked to actually have the nerve to do it."

Have mercy, she was cute. "Here," he said, reaching for her hand. "I'll help." A tiny tremor rippled from her hand to his, and he smiled. "Hey, don't be so scared. You'd think I was a wild animal or something."

She laughed at that. "You're saying you won't bite?"

"I won't bite." He brought her fingers to his face.

She leaned toward him, her sweet apple scent filling the air as she brought her other hand to his face as well, then eased her fingertips across his forehead. Her eyes were mere inches from his, but she couldn't see a thing; instead, those eyes appeared to be studying, memorizing details as her thumbs ran gently across his brows.

"You always had thick brows," she said, and gave him an easy smile.

"That a good thing?" he asked, closing his eyes as her perusal moved to his eyelids.

"Yes," she whispered, while she softly caressed his lids and lashes. "And long lashes too. I remember them. Long, dark brown lashes."

"You told me back then that you thought it was a sin for a guy to have long lashes."

She laughed. "Yeah, I said that, and I meant it." She touched his cheeks, traced his jawline. "Smile," she said.

Landon did as she asked, as if he wouldn't give her anything she requested now, and Georgie ran a finger across the indention beneath each cheek.

"My mother said they should outlaw the Cutter dimples."

"Did she now?" Landon asked, smiling broader.

"Yes, she did." She eased a single finger across his mouth.

Landon noticed her breathing grow deeper, and saw that she moistened her lips when she touched his mouth. He wanted so badly to kiss her, but he wasn't certain if this was the right time. And he didn't want to interrupt her while she was obviously studying everything about him. So he held his desire in check and waited while her hands slid to his hair, then pushed through.

"Your hair *is* shorter now."

"Kind of goes along with the whole army thing," he said jokingly.

"I like it," she said. "It's odd, I always thought your hair would be soft and silky, but it's more coarse and kind of springy, isn't it?"

"Yeah, I guess it is."

"I don't think I ever touched it in high school. Isn't that funny? I mean, you wouldn't think about it back then, but we never really touched, did we? A hug every now and then, but nothing like this, huh?"

"Trust me, if you'd have ever touched me like this, I'd remember it," he said, and was rewarded by a sweet flush of pink to her cheeks.

"Still charming," she said softly.

"I try."

Then she chewed her lower lip again, and her hands moved to the sides of his neck before her palms slid across his shoulders and down his arms. He heard a tiny gasp when she reached his biceps.

"What is it?" he asked.

"You're, well, really muscled now, aren't you?"

He laughed. He couldn't help it. "Georgiana Sanders, you're doing amazing things to my ego."

She took her hands from him and said, "I probably should stop now."

He nodded, "Yeah, you probably should." Her touch was way too tempting, and even though he knew he wouldn't take things too far, it never was good to tempt himself too much.

"But there's one more thing," she said.

"What is it?"

"Can you put my hand on your tattoo? The one for your friends?"

Nothing she could have asked him would have touched his heart more. "Of course." He moved her hand to his inner wrist then guided it along the path of the tattoo. "This is where the image starts, with their death dates. And then here is the rifle," he trailed her finger across the gun's length, "and the helmet." Again, he moved her finger along the path and found a shiver of sentimentality covering him as he shared the meaningful emblem. "The dog tags are here."

"It's so sad," she whispered, as a teardrop fell from her eyes to land in the center of the death dates on his arm. Then she dabbed at her cheeks and looked up at him, astonishment clearly etched on her features. "I'm crying."

Landon wiped another tear from her cheek. "It's okay, Georgie. I know they're in a better place."

"You don't understand," she said, shaking her head. "I haven't cried in a very long time. Years. I haven't been able to."

"You haven't been able to cry?"

"No," she said. "I—I fought it for years, because Pete said how horrible I looked when I cried, that it made me even less appealing. So I fought tears. And then, after a while, I stopped being able to cry anymore." Her lashes were spiked from tears now, and even more droplets steadily fell down her cheeks. But she wasn't frowning anymore; she'd actually started to smile. "But I'm crying now, with you."

Landon's anger bristled through him, but he controlled the impulse to tell her exactly what he thought of his old friend right now. Instead, he wrapped an arm around her and pulled her close. "I know this is going to sound odd," he said, "but I'm glad I made you cry."

"Doesn't sound any more odd than me saying I'm glad you got shot." They laughed and her tears slowed. She brushed the final one away before turning her face to his. "This afternoon has meant the world to me, Landon."

"It's meant the world to me too," he said. She had no idea how much this had meant, to see her laugh again and even to see her cry, especially since he now knew those tears meant that she was breaking free of Pete's attempt to degrade her.

Thank You, God.

She shivered in his arms. "Landon, it feels like it's getting late."

"Yeah, the sun's heading down quick. We should probably get started back before it gets…" He stopped short when he realized what he'd been about to say. But she'd already completed the thought.

"Before it gets dark?" She gave him a soft grin. "It's okay. I don't want you trying to watch everything you say in front of me. You would be surprised how many times people ask me if I want to *see* something." She shrugged. "No one says it to offend me, and I don't take it that way. I promise."

"Still…"

"Abi says it all the time. Doesn't bother me, except when I think about how much I do want to see whatever it is she has to show me. Usually I can tell a lot about her crafts, her toys, or whatever by touch. And she seems to like describing everything to me. I think it makes her feel important." She stood, and Landon did as well. "Come on, let's walk back. Abi's probably wanting to tell me about her riding lesson."

They made their way back through the trail quicker than they had found their way to the ridge, with Georgie taking her steps assuredly rather than timidly like before. Landon attributed the boost of confidence to their talk and said another silent prayer of thanks to God for letting her feel comfortable with him again.

As they neared the house, sure enough, Abi waited by the barn and started yelling and waving as they came into view. A few feet from her granddaughter, Eden looked up from brushing Fallon and smiled at Landon.

Abi darted toward them at a full run. "Momma, I did so good! Grandma said so! She thinks I might be ready to ride the trails soon, like you used to do. Do you think you're ready to ride again too? Do you want to go on the trails with me?" She wrapped her arms around Georgiana with such force that Landon thought the two might topple.

Georgiana laughed. "Slow down, Abi. Take a breath."

"I will, but I'm so excited. I'm going to ride the

trails!" She looked to Landon. "And Grandma said maybe you would want to come too and bring your horse and help Momma ride too. Would you want to do that? Go riding with me and with Momma? You are going to come, aren't you, Momma?"

"I don't think I have a choice." Georgiana squeezed her daughter and smothered her face in Abi's curls. "Yes, I'd like to come. Soon I'll go ride the trails with you. I promise."

Abi smiled to her cheeks. "I love you, Momma."

"I love you too."

"Landon, did you walk over here?" Eden asked, glancing at the darkening sky.

"Yes, I did, and I should probably head back while I can still see the path."

"I could give you a ride over, if you want," Eden offered. "Or you could take Fallon or Sugar, if you like."

"Nah," Landon said. "I think I'll walk."

"Want a flashlight?" Abi asked. "We've got a bunch of flashlights in the barn. I could get you one. Do you want a black one or a red one or a blue one?"

Landon grinned at the sweet little girl, so much like her mother. "I don't think I'll take one this time, Abi. But thank you."

"Okay, if you're sure," Abi said.

"Hey, Abi, how about if it doesn't rain tomorrow, you and me and your mom can go walking on the trails, so you'll know the routes we're going to take when we ride. I bet we might even see some animals on the path."

"What kind of animals?"

"Oh, you never know. I'd guess squirrels, chipmunks, maybe a fox. And maybe even a baby rabbit."

"A baby rabbit? I'd love to see a baby bunny! I saw some rabbits at the zoo, but they were big. I haven't seen a baby one."

"Then we'll go looking for one tomorrow if the weather is good," he said.

"Okay!" she said excitedly.

"Abi, why don't you come help me finish up?" Eden nodded toward the barn.

"I'll see you tomorrow, Mr. Landon. And don't forget about us going to look for those animals. Especially that bunny. Okay?"

"Okay."

"What time will you get here?"

"I don't get off of work until 3:00, and then I've got a few things to do around the farm. How about 5:00?"

"Okay!" Abi darted into the barn after her grandmother saying, "Did you hear that, Grandma? Mr. Landon is coming tomorrow at 5:00. Make sure I remember to be ready at 5:00!"

"Oh, I feel certain you won't forget," Eden said, her voice fading as they moved farther into the barn.

"You sure you don't want a flashlight?" Georgie asked.

He glanced up. The sun was barely visible, and it'd be pitch black soon, nothing but the stars to guide him through the trails. "Yeah, I'm sure. You see, there's this very special person who has to navigate the dark at all times, and I want a chance to see the world the way she sees it."

She smiled. "Well, in case you're wondering, she sees it a little brighter today, thanks to you."

Chapter Twelve

"Ooh, look, I see it." Abi's attempt at a whisper was so pitiful that Georgiana nearly laughed out loud, but Landon sounded completely serious when he responded.

"See how fuzzy his hair looks now?" he whispered back, squeezing Georgiana's hand when he spoke. "As he gets older, it'll look more like regular rabbit hair and not just fuzzy."

"How do you know it's a boy?" Abi asked. "'Cause he's brown?"

"No," Landon said, still as serious as before, without a hint of laughter or mockery in his tone, "I'm guessing. It could be a girl."

"Oh, okay," Abi said, her whisper a little better now. "Well, I think its face is sweet, like a girl's face. So I think she's a girl, and I'm gonna name her Trixie."

"That's a great name," Landon said.

Georgiana stood rock still while she listened to the exchange. Obviously they had finally located the tiny bunny—or one of its brothers or sisters—and she certainly didn't want to ruin the moment for Abi. They'd had to wait through two rainy days before they'd been able to take on the trails, and Abi had even forgone her Saturday morning cartoons to get an early start.

The wait hadn't been too bad though, because Landon had followed through with his promise of coming over to visit every day. Consequently, he, Georgiana and Abi had spent the past two afternoons playing games on the front porch while the rain fell all around them. It'd been soothing and enjoyable, with lots of laughter and plenty of fun. The way family time should be, in Georgiana's opinion. And it'd made her realize that she and Abi had never had *real* family fun before. Then Landon had stayed each night for dinner and had seamlessly become a regular fixture in Abi's world…and in Georgiana's.

She could really get used to this, had already begun to get used to it, truth be told.

"Oh, there she goes," Abi said. "Look at the cute way she hops. Can we follow her?"

"Nah, we should probably let her go find her burrow and see her momma. We'll look for her again next time we're on the trail."

"Okay," Abi said, her voice back to normal volume now. "Mom, we saw the cutest bunny. It was light brown and fuzzy, but it's gonna have regular hair one day. Did you hear?"

"Yes, I did," Georgiana said, happy to be included in the conversation. She understood that there were times that she simply couldn't be included due to her inability to see, but her sweet daughter always drew her into the event as soon as possible. And Georgiana loved her even more because of it. "She was cute?"

"Oh, yes, Mommy. She was *so* cute! I think I'd like to have a bunny. Do you think Grandma would want a bunny at the barn?"

"I'm sure she would probably be fine with it," Georgiana said.

"Your grandmother let your mom keep rabbits when she was little. One of my favorite parts of coming over to visit was getting to play with them. You know, I bet she may still have that old rabbit hutch out in the barn. We'll look for it when we get back, and if your grandma says it's okay, I can pick you up some rabbits from the Claremont Trade Day next Friday."

"*Some* rabbits?" Georgiana asked. "I thought we were talking about one bunny."

"Don't you remember, Georgiana," Landon

started, "how you wanted your rabbit to have playmates? I'm sure Abi feels the same way."

"Oh, yes!" Abi said. "I want my rabbit to have lots of friends."

"And don't *you* remember, Landon," Georgiana asked, "that my three rabbits turned into over thirty rabbits at the speed of light?"

"Of course I remember. Abi should experience that fun too." He barely hid his laughter in the words. Those rabbits would take over the farm, but it would be fun.

Georgiana grinned. "I can't help but remember all of those white cotton balls all over the farm and how they kept my mother running ragged."

"We'll help take care of them," Landon said.

"So I can get a *bunch* of rabbits?" Abi asked excitedly.

"I'll get a couple," Landon said, "and we'll see what happens."

"If your couple ends up being male and female, we know what'll happen," Georgiana said.

"What'll happen?" Abi asked.

"You'll have that bunch of bunnies you're wanting," Landon said. "Pretty soon."

"Great!" Abi cheered, and Georgiana laughed.

"I better prepare Mom," she said.

"You think she'd tell Abi no?" Landon asked.

"Definitely not, but I still want to warn her of what's coming."

"Grandma won't care. She likes animals," Abi said.

"Yes, she does," Landon agreed.

"I think horses are her favorite, but I bet she likes rabbits too. Hey, Mommy, did you think some more about going on the horses today? Yesterday you said you'd think about it, remember? Grandma said since she doesn't have the riding lessons on Saturdays that we can take Fallon. And Mr. Landon brought Sam. We could come back up here on the horses and do the trails and keep looking for more bunnies and stuff."

Abi had made this request no less than ten times since Eden mentioned the idea yesterday. Landon had been oddly silent each time Abi begged, and Georgiana wasn't certain that was because he thought she wasn't ready to try riding again or because he didn't want to interfere in Georgiana's parenting. Either way, Georgiana had already decided that if Abi asked again, she wouldn't let her daughter down.

"Tell you what, let's see what Landon thinks about us doing the trails together today." He still held her hand, so she turned to face him and said, "Well, what do you think?"

"Honestly?"

"Yes, tell me the truth," she said, as though she'd want him to be anything less than honest. "Do you think I could try, with your help?"

"I don't think there are too many things you can't do, Georgie," he said softly, "with or without my help. And I will be with you to lead you, but I'm betting Fallon could probably ride you through the trails with *her* eyes closed."

Georgiana laughed. "You know, she probably could." Then she said to Abi, "Okay, little girl. Looks like you're going to get your wish."

"You're going to ride? With me and Mr. Landon? On the trails and everything?"

"I'm going to try."

Evidently Georgiana was more nervous about riding than she'd realized, because she didn't hear a single bit of the excited conversation that took place between Abi and Landon during the walk back to the barn. And she barely heard Landon's instructions as he saddled Fallon and prepared her to ride. Instead, one thing kept repeating through her head, her own silent mantra.

I'm going to ride again. I'm going to ride again. I'm going to ride again!

"Georgiana? Honey, are you okay?" Her mother's voice crept through the silent chant and Georgiana blinked.

"Okay?" she asked.

"Yes. Landon is trying to help you up."

Landon's low chuckle soothed her nerves. "It's easier to ride when you're in the saddle," he said, then squeezed her hand. The simple action sent a warmth of awareness up her arm and a boost of confidence to her soul. Landon believed she could do this. Landon believed in her. "You ready?" he asked.

She was *so* ready. "Yes."

"Okay, I'm going to help you up." He placed his hand on her calf. He had one arm around her waist, the other guiding her foot to the stirrup, and the close proximity, the intimateness of the motions of him lifting her and helping her into the saddle, gave her a swift rush of exhilaration. Yes, she was excited to be riding again. But being this close to Landon—that excited her just as much, or more.

The next thing she knew, she was on Fallon, as comfortable in the saddle as if she'd never stopped riding at all. She leaned forward and ran her palm down Fallon's neck. "Hey, girl, it's me."

"Oh, believe me," Eden said, "she knows."

Landon handed her the reins. "Everything feel good? Stirrups okay?"

"Everything feels great." And *she* felt great, here with him.

"Wow, Mom, you look so pretty on Fallon!"

Abi's voice was near, and Georgiana realized her daughter was already ready to go.

"Are you on Sugar?" she asked.

"No, I'm riding on Sam with Mr. Landon." She laughed. "Remember, he said I should ride with him this first time, and I said okay."

Georgiana assumed that was a portion of the conversation she'd missed when she'd been so absorbed in the idea of riding again. "Right. Well, that's a good idea, for you to ride with him today."

"I'll ride by myself soon, though, right? Like maybe next time we go?"

"Right," Landon said. "Maybe even next time."

"This is gonna be fun, huh, Mommy?"

"Yes," Georgiana said, "it is." It already was.

"Fallon knows the trails," Eden said quietly to Georgiana. "She should follow along without any troubles at all. She rarely ever spooks, only for…"

"Extremely loud thunder, screams…and snakes," Georgiana said. "Don't worry, Mom. I remember everything about riding Fallon. And there's no rain in the forecast for today, right?"

"No, no rain," her mother said.

"And I'm sure Landon will warn me if he sees anything slithering nearby."

"You can count on it," Landon said.

"Ew, I don't like snakes," Abi said. "Let's don't talk about snakes. Let's talk about bunnies."

Landon laughed. "That's a deal."

"Be careful," Eden said, still speaking softly to Georgiana. "I know you're ready, but I guess— well, a mother never stops worrying about her child. But more than being worried for you, I'm happy for you. I know how much you want this, honey."

"I do," Georgiana agreed. "And don't worry. I'm sure Fallon still knows all of the trails, but I remember the trails too, you know."

"I know," her mother said, "I just meant…"

"I know what you meant, but I feel good about this. Everything is going to be fine."

"Let me get you a riding helmet," her mother said.

"We all have to wear helmets in our class," Abi pointed out. "Mine's pink. I'm wearing it already. Mr. Landon, are you gonna wear one? We've got blue and black and green ones. Those are boy colors."

"I think I'm just gonna wear my hat this time."

Georgiana remembered the springy texture of his hair against her fingers, and the well-chiseled planes of his face, the strong jawline, the cheekbones, full mouth, long lashes. She thought of the entire combination of Landon Cutter's face beneath the brim of a Stetson, and she wished that she could see him now, sitting on top of Sam with her daughter in front of him in the saddle. The vision touched her heart.

"Mommy, do you want a helmet?" Abi continued.

"Yes, I'd love a helmet." Georgiana swallowed past the lump in her throat. Soon she felt the hard fiberglass shell against her hand.

"Here you go, honey," her mother said, and Georgiana took the helmet and strapped it on.

"Yours is white, Mommy. I like pink for me, but white is pretty for you."

"Thanks, sweetie."

"Now Georgiana, you remember if you want Fallon to stop, you just…"

"Hold my breath," Georgiana said, running a hand along Fallon's mane. "I remember, Mom. Fallon's the best horse around, aren't you, girl?"

"That's why she's so amazing for my classes, but the *reason* she's the best horse around is because she had a great little girl to train her and love her, make her care about whoever is riding her at all times."

"Are you talking about Mommy?" Abi asked. "Mommy trained Fallon?"

"Yes, dear, she did."

"Wow, cool!" Abi said, while Georgiana listened to Landon bringing Sam to her left.

"Ready to go?" he asked.

She hesitated, and Fallon stiffened, obviously sensing her nervousness. But she couldn't help it; her fears were creeping back in, along with Pete's warning that she'd fall off and leave Abi with "even less of a mother."

Landon lowered his voice. "You can do this, Georgie. I have faith in you."

Such a contrast to what she'd heard from her *ex*-husband. "You know what?" she said.

"What?"

"I have faith in me too."

"That's what I'm talking about. You ready, Abi?"

"Yep, I'm ready."

"Okay, we'll go side by side till we get to the trail. Then Abi and I will lead, and you can follow, Georgiana. I think that should work well for Fallon, don't you think?"

"Fallon will know what to do," Georgiana said assuredly.

"And we aren't in any kind of race. We'll just be walking the trails. Is that okay with you, Abi?"

"Yep, I can look at more stuff if we're going slow. And we won't scare the bunnies."

"Right, we won't scare the bunnies." Landon touched a hand to Georgiana's tight grip on the reins. "It'll be fine. Fallon is ready and listening for your instructions. You're in control, and you're going to do great."

"Thanks," she said. "So we should go?"

"As soon as you're ready."

She nodded, gently tapped her leg against Fallon's side and clicked the roof of her mouth. "Okay, Fallon, let's walk."

Fallon started walking, and Georgiana listened to her mother saying goodbye, to the sound of the horses' hooves against the earth, to Abi's laughter, to Landon's encouraging words, to birds chirping, cows mooing, chickens clucking. She'd heard many of these everyday noises nonstop since returning to the farm, but something about listening to the medley as she sat on Fallon's back made it seem more real. Made her feel more alive.

"Georgie, are you okay?" Landon asked.

"Mommy? Are you crying?"

Her tears fell so steadily that they passed down her cheek and continued down her neck, but Georgiana didn't wipe them away. They were a sign, a sign that everything was different now. She was riding again. She was having fun with her daughter and enjoying time with a man—with Landon. And she was crying. Not tears of sadness, but tears of joy. "Yes, sweetie, I'm crying. But they're happy tears. Very, very happy tears."

Chapter Thirteen

Landon rode Sam ahead of Georgiana and Fallon as they made their way across the field toward the pond. Eden had taken Abi shopping for school supplies after church, and Landon wanted to take advantage of time alone with Georgiana. He'd suggested they ride the horses to the pond. Her smile as she sat astride Fallon and crossed the field let him know this was a good idea.

He'd hoped she'd come to church with Eden and Abi this morning, but he hadn't really expected her to show. She was still apprehensive about being around those who knew her before her blindness, and Landon knew her anxiety wasn't as much due to the way people acted around her as it was to the way Pete had told her they acted. She had to be encouraged to get back out again, and he knew it'd take time. But that didn't stop him from wanting to let her know she was missed.

"Brother Henry had a great lesson today," he said.

She ran her teeth across her lower lip and gripped Fallon's reins a little tighter.

Landon wasn't giving up that easily. He knew how much church had meant to Georgiana, and he thought worshipping with fellow Christians again would help her more than anything. "I think you'd have enjoyed it, Brother Henry's lesson. He talked about renewed faith." When she didn't say anything, he added, "I'd have liked for you to have been there...with me."

"I thought about going this morning," she said, so softly he nearly didn't hear.

"You did?" Landon tried not to sound too surprised.

"Abi's recital is less than two weeks away, so it won't be long until I have to get out of the house again. I'm feeling more confident about the whole idea of going out in public. I mean, if I can saddle a horse on my own and ride, surely I can handle venturing around town and going to church. I mean, I know I can do it, it's just that I can't stand the awkwardness when people don't know what to say around me."

Landon knew how she felt, but for a different reason. "I hadn't realized it before now, but I get the same kind of reaction sometimes, especially when I'm wearing my fatigues. People want to acknowledge my service, but they aren't quite sure what to say. I can tell though, by the way they look at me."

"I can tell by the way they move out of the way," she said. "Or get really quiet."

For the first time, he understood what she felt, and he thought he knew how to help her deal with it. "The thing is, they aren't acting odd because they look down on me, or on you, they're usually just trying not to say the wrong thing, do the wrong thing. They don't want to offend you in any way, Georgie."

Her head tilted as though considering his words. "But I *am* different."

"And in a way, so am I. Every soldier comes back different than he or she was before. The experience changes you, and your experience has changed you. But you're still the same Georgie."

"And you're still the same Landon." She smiled, a real smile that claimed her entire face and shone from within. "I have missed Brother Henry's sermons. He's an excellent speaker and applies the Bible so well to everyday living. I need that now. Maybe I'll try to go next Sunday."

Her words touched Landon's heart, because he couldn't help but think he'd been a part of this change. "That'd be great, Georgie."

"I let myself get down because of the accident,

because of the blindness." She paused. "And because of Pete. But I now know that I shouldn't hide from life. How will I ever be a real mom to Abi if I'm never with her for the important moments? She'll be making memories, and I won't be in them. I can't let that happen, not anymore."

"Exactly." He looked ahead and spotted the pond. "We're nearly there."

"I thought so," she said. "It'll take me a while to judge distance around the fields again, especially when I'm riding, but lucky for me Fallon knows her way everywhere."

He dismounted then moved to help her down. "Here, let me help." Reaching for her hand, Landon guided her out of the saddle. He'd helped her before, but Abi and Eden had always been nearby, so he'd released his hold when her feet hit the ground. This time, however, it was just the two of them in the open field, standing by the pond, and Landon didn't let her go. On the contrary, he ran his hands up her arms and enjoyed the feel of her smooth skin against his palms. "I'm glad you agreed to ride with me today."

She moistened her lips, and those hazel eyes appeared to be searching, looking for something. Looking for him. "I'm glad you asked me."

"Georgie, I want you to trust me, and I believe you're starting to. But I need you to know that you can, that you can count on me never to intentionally hurt you and never to leave you." He wanted her to know that she wouldn't go through what Pete had put her through again, not with him. "And you can open up to me, tell me your fears, tell me your dreams. I want us to be that close again."

Her brows dipped, mouth tugged down at the edges, and Landon wondered if he'd said something wrong. "What is it?"

A tear pushed free and she wiped it away. "It's just that I haven't been able to trust like that in a very long time, but I want to. And I'll try to… with you."

A breeze filtered through her curls, and she blinked as a wayward lock brushed against her face. Landon tenderly slid the curl away, and then just as tenderly brushed his fingertips along her face, finally cupping her chin in his hands and tilting her face toward his.

"Georgiana," he whispered, unsure of whether he needed to ask permission or whether she would even welcome his kiss. But he didn't have to ask.

She eased her lips closer, slid her eyes closed and whispered, "Please."

Many times in Afghanistan he'd remembered the emotion behind that kiss in the church. He'd believed he'd never experience anything that powerful again. Until now.

Georgiana's mouth was soft and welcoming, her hands trembling as they found his face and then slid around his neck to draw him closer. Landon didn't want the kiss to end, didn't want this closeness to end, and when they did finally part, he realized that he'd probably kissed her a little longer than a first kiss would have warranted, because she touched her lips and then laughed.

"Well," she whispered.

"Well?"

"Well...wow."

He grinned. "I've been gone a while, Georgie. I guess I've had a decent kiss coming."

"That was only 'decent'?" she questioned teasingly, and he loved the way she joked with him. She was growing more and more comfortable around him every day.

"Okay, a spectacular kiss coming."

"That's more like it," she said, as a loud splash drew his attention to the pond. He'd thought he'd heard a couple of splashes while they were kissing too, but he'd been too absorbed in the moment to pay too much attention.

"Was that a fish?"

"Yes," she said, still laughing from their flirting. "Daddy stocked the pond when I was a little girl, and evidently the fish have only increased. Abi and I have heard them jumping every time we're out here."

"I wonder if our pond has that many fish. I know it did when we were little, but we were too busy as teens to spend a lot of time fishing. And I know John and Casey have probably been too busy as well."

"I asked Abi about going fishing the other day, but she wasn't overly thrilled about baiting her hook or touching a fish," she said with a grin. "I think it'd be great though if she could enjoy—" Georgie's mouth dropped open and she clapped her hands together. "That's it! That's what you and John need to do!"

"What?"

"Didn't your property have fishing cabins on it? Over by the pond?"

"We actually call them fishing shacks, but yeah, they're still there. John mentioned that he'd started to fix them up to rent them out but he didn't get finished. Why?"

"How close is he to having them ready?" Her excitement was palpable.

"I have no idea. Ready for what?"

"Think about it. If your pond is stocked like this one, or even if it isn't, you could stock it by the spring, and that's when your business would need to open, right? Isn't that what Andy Cothran said? He just needs to see a business plan and proof that you're making an effort to get the business up and running. You wouldn't have to have everything in working order until the spring." She nodded and smiled. "That's plenty of time to get a fishing camp together." Before Landon could say anything, she continued, "It'd be really good if you could have a grand opening around spring break, when all the kids are out of school. Think how much fun that would be!"

"A fishing camp?" The only kind of fishing camps Landon knew of were the dilapidated shacks in the more swampy areas of the state, and they were typically only used by old men who wanted a weekend away from their wives and kids.

Georgiana must have followed his train of thought because she shook her head. "Not the kind of fishing camp you're used to," she said, "but a camp for kids. You wouldn't want it to be a summer camp, because that limits what you can do the rest of the year. I think it should be a weekend camp, where parents and their children could come rent a cabin for a weekend and have some quality time together, away from the hustle and bustle of computers and cell phones and the world and just relax…and fish."

The more excited she got, the faster she talked,

just like the Georgie he knew before, and he loved not only seeing her so excited but also the entire idea she presented. "A fishing camp," he repeated.

She nodded. "Yes, and you need to get John working on that business plan right now, and probably should check out those cabins to see if he's done enough work on them to impress Andy at the bank, or if we need to do more."

Landon's heart beat a little faster at her mention of *we*. She was already including herself in his world, and he couldn't be more pleased. "Well, why don't we ride over and check them out now? John's probably at the house. We can stop and see if he wants to ride out to the shacks too."

"Cabins," she corrected.

Landon laughed. "Right. Cabins."

Within minutes, they were back in the saddles and riding to Landon's farm. But this time, they didn't walk; they galloped. And Georgiana looked as comfortable in the saddle as she had when she was a teen, when she could see. Her long hair bounced against her back and her laugh echoed through the air as they crossed the fields. The horses slowed when they reached the wooded trails, but Georgiana's occasional giddy laugh continued until they reached Landon's property and found John standing outside the barn texting on his phone.

"Well, aren't you a sight for sore eyes?" John said to Georgiana. "Can't remember the last time I saw you on Fallon."

"Landon helped me start riding again," Georgiana said.

"I know. He told me, and it sure didn't take you long to get comfortable, huh?"

"No, it didn't, but I had a good teacher."

John's phone beeped, and he started texting again. "I'm talking to the lady from Chicago." He tapped a few keys, then hit the send button. "I know we can't present the dude ranch idea as our business plan, but I still think it'd work. Just doing a little more research. I've had a couple of ideas about other businesses we could give to Andy by the end of the month, but nothing that I think will really fly."

"Well, it just so happens that's why we're here. Georgie had an idea that just might work, depending on where you stand on fixing up the fishing shacks."

"Fishing cabins," she said again, smiling.

"I've got to get used to that," Landon said. "Tell him, Georgie."

He listened as she described her idea to John and could tell his brother also thought it was a good one.

"And fishing is something that Andy would

have to be on board with," John said after he heard Georgiana's plan. "I mean, we've got the Bowers fishing hole, and it stays packed, but it's more of a single-day fishing thing, nothing like this, where people from out of town could come and stay in one of the cabins and really enjoy some privacy on our farm." He grinned. "I like it! And I can already think of how I'd present it in a business plan. It just so happens we're already discussing business plans in my Intro to Business Research class. Might as well put what I'm learning into action." His phone beeped again, and he tapped another series of keys. "I'll get Dana's opinion on the fishing camp idea too. Maybe she'll know something to include in the business plan that'll really make it shine."

"Dana?" Landon questioned.

"The business lady from Chicago."

Landon smirked. It didn't take John long to get on a first-name basis with the woman he'd never met. John caught the look and shook his head. "She's really helpful," he said.

"Obviously," Landon said, while Georgiana smothered a laugh.

"So, are the cabins habitable?" she asked.

"I wouldn't say that," John said. "I've swept them out and started cleaning them up, but I'd imagine we'd want to fix them up nice if we planned on bringing in tourists. Reckon we could fix one up rather quick so we could show Andy what we have in mind?"

"We've got a lot of things in storage in our attic," Georgiana said. "I brought back furniture from Tampa that I don't need anymore. You can use anything you want. I know there's a bed and a dresser. Maybe a small kitchen table and chairs."

"Well, everything about the shacks—cabins—is small, so we wouldn't need much," Landon said. "Plus, if we go for the rustic appeal, maybe provide a wood-burning stove and lanterns instead of trying to get electricity out there, that'd help speed the time we need for fixing everything up."

"That's a good idea," John said.

"And I think keeping it as natural and outdoorsy as possible is the way to go," Georgiana said. "I think Abi would love it. Any child would."

"I agree. So, you want to ride out to the cabins with us and pick the one that we want to tackle first?" Landon waited for John to send yet another text.

"Yeah, I do." John moved to saddle up his horse, and his phone beeped in the interim. He glanced at the display. "Dana thinks the fishing camp is a good idea too."

"Well then, by all means, we have to do it," Landon said with a grin.

John ignored his sarcasm, mounted Red and headed into the field. "Come on!"

"You with us?" Landon asked Georgiana.

"I'm ready," she said, smiling broadly and warming his heart with her enthusiasm. How could she think her blindness limited her in the world, limited her usefulness to others—her usefulness to him? She'd probably just put them on a path to save their farm. And won a little more of his heart in the process.

Chapter Fourteen

In late August and early September, Alabama often received a few unseasonal days of windy, cool weather due to the tropical storms prevalent in the Gulf of Mexico and the Atlantic. This year was no different, and the day of Abi's piano recital was particularly breezy and cool. Rain had been predicted, but as of yet hadn't made an appearance. Consequently, the weather was perfect for the event, as if God was encouraging Georgiana to take this step, leave the house, support her daughter and start living again.

She'd spent the past two weeks busier than she'd been in years, doing her transcriptions during the day and spending the afternoons with Abi and Landon. Abi had jumped on board with the fishing-cabin decorating project, particularly when she realized the ride on the horses to get to Landon's cabins was farther than her trips to the pond. And

Georgiana had become so accustomed to riding again that she and Abi rode over on their own one day when Landon had to work late at the feed store. John, of course, watched for their arrival but still...Georgiana had done it, ridden the trails on her own with her little girl without any mishaps. Her confidence soared like it hadn't in years.

She stepped into the red dress, slipped on the "cute" shoes Mandy had helped them pick out that night at the square and wondered if she looked half as pretty as she felt. Because Landon made her feel pretty, beautiful even. Their alone time together over the past two weeks had been special and sensual and *right*. Georgiana felt feminine around him, desirable around him, *loved* around him, even if he hadn't yet said the *L* word.

Naturally, the realization of how Landon made her feel brought to mind the contrast in Landon and Pete, along with the reminder that Pete was on his way to Claremont for Abi's recital. Tonight would be her first time to be around him since the divorce, and Georgiana prayed that she didn't let him bring her down again.

God, be with me tonight. Stay with me. Give me the courage to face him and not let him beat me down.

She thought about what else she wanted to find the courage to do tonight. *And please, Lord, let me finally tell Landon everything about my blindness. If it be Your will, let him understand why I didn't tell him before, and please—please—don't let him blame himself.* Their relationship was growing stronger at a rapid pace, but her secret was an obstacle that couldn't remain if they were going to have anything long-term. Secrets had no place in a marriage, and she wished with all her heart that she'd simply told him the truth in the beginning. But she hadn't. And now she had to pray that he'd forgive her for never opening up.

From now on, I'll tell him everything, Lord. But let him forgive me this time, please.

"Georgiana, we're ready to go," Eden called.

"Momma, are you coming? We can't be late!"

"I'm coming," she said, gathering her courage for whatever awaited her tonight and then heading downstairs to meet her mom and daughter.

"Wow, you look like a real princess!" Abi's sweet words gave her a boost of confidence.

"Thanks, sweetie. I'm sure you do too."

"I do! Grandma said so."

Georgiana laughed, and Eden did as well.

"Okay, we need to head on to the square. Landon's meeting us there, right?" Eden asked.

"Yes. He's done at the feed store but he still needed to shower. He said he should get there not long after we arrive." Georgiana hoped Pete wasn't at the gallery already. Abi had to get there early to get in her position for performing, but the actual recital wouldn't start for another hour. An hour with Pete wasn't something Georgiana wanted.

They drove to the gallery with Abi chattering nonstop about everything from the piece she'd be playing to the type of punch Mrs. Camp said they'd have to the way her shoes made her feet feel "glittery." Finally, they arrived at the gallery, parked the car, and then Abi's final statement left no room for doubt that Pete had already arrived.

"Daddy's here!" she said, bounding from the car as soon as it stopped and before Eden or Georgiana could tell her to slow down.

"Is he alone?" Georgiana whispered.

"No, dear. He's definitely not alone." Eden's tone told Georgiana plenty. Not only had Pete brought his fiancée, Tanya, but evidently the woman drew attention.

"Pretty?" Georgiana asked, and then wished she didn't care.

"Well now, you know Pete," her mother said. "But I can tell you right now, she doesn't hold a candle to you." She patted a hand on Georgiana's knee.

"Thanks, Mom." Any mother would have told her daughter the same thing, regardless of how the other woman looked. Even so, her words did make

Georgiana feel better. A little. But what would really make her feel better was if she wasn't alone. If only…

"Hey."

"Landon!" As if he'd materialized from her very thoughts, he'd opened her car door and placed her hand in his.

"Sorry I ran late. At least I made it in time."

"Perfect timing, I'd say," Eden said.

"Me too." Georgiana climbed out of the car and let him lead her toward the gallery. With Landon by her side she could handle Pete. She could handle meeting Tanya, if she had to. In fact, she could handle anything. "Thanks."

He didn't ask what for. "Wouldn't have it any other way." He wrapped an arm around her and whispered, "He's standing at the door, and he's got a brunette beside him. Are you ready?"

"I am now." And it made her feel amazing that her words were true.

"Three shallow brick steps to the top," Landon whispered as they apparently neared the entrance to Gina Brown's Art Gallery.

Georgiana appreciated the fact that he subtly helped her blend in public. They'd been together so much over the past few weeks that he'd learned when she needed help as well as when she didn't, and he helped her lovingly. Unlike the man who apparently stood at the top of these steps.

"Georgiana." Pete's tone held the contempt she'd heard throughout the majority of their marriage.

"Hello, Pete."

"Hi! I'm Tanya! I'm pleased to meet you! We're looking forward to having Abi in our wedding!" She yelled every syllable, and Georgiana fought the impulse to tell the girl that she was blind, not deaf.

"Tanya, there's no reason to yell," Pete said sternly, and Georgiana realized that this poor girl was already getting a dose of the "real" Pete Watson.

Run. Now.

"Cutter. What are you doing here?" Pete's voice dripped venom.

"In the States? Or here? I'm in the States because I finished my tour of duty. I'm here because I want to hear Abi's performance…with Georgiana."

"Unbelievable," Pete said.

"What's that?" Landon asked.

Georgiana had no idea what Pete might say and she certainly didn't want to draw a scene in public. Her whole goal for the evening was to blend and not embarrass Abi. If Pete caused a scene, then that would embarrass their little girl, and she wasn't about to let that happen. "Let's go sit down, Landon."

"Come on, Tanya, we'll go get a good seat too… so we can *see*."

Georgiana was certain she didn't imagine his emphasis on the last word, and from the low snarl she heard from Landon, he'd detected it as well.

"What you ever saw in him…" Landon started.

"I have no idea," she finished, and was rewarded with a low chuckle.

"Well, he's sitting on the opposite side of the room, so for now, we're home free. And by the way, if you wanted to blend with your surroundings tonight, you missed the mark." He led her to a row of chairs and they sat down.

"I did?"

Before she had a chance to panic too long wondering why, he added, "Yes, because there's no way you can blend looking like that, in that dress and with your hair all curled and tumbling like a red waterfall down your back. You're stunning, Georgiana, and you definitely stand out."

She could feel her blush flame her cheeks. "Landon."

"Only telling the truth," he said. "And I'm fairly certain I'm the envy of every man in here…including the one who lost you."

"Oh, Landon, I—" she paused her words before

she blurted out the rest for whoever was sitting around to hear. They hadn't confessed their love, but she knew in her heart that she loved him, really loved him, and the natural urge to tell him was nearly overpowering. But she needed to tell him her secret first, about the cause of her blindness, get everything out in the open so they could start fresh, start new, and build something that would last a lifetime. Because that's what she knew for certain that she wanted, a lifetime with Landon.

"You...what, Georgie?" His voice was a breathy whisper against her ear. He knew. She had no doubt he knew what she'd been about to say, and he was teasing her now.

She swallowed. "I'll—tell you later."

He leaned closer, softly kissed the shell of her ear. "I hope you do."

"Okay if I sit by y'all?" Her mother had already taken Abi backstage.

Georgiana prayed the lights were low enough that Eden didn't see her flaming cheeks. "Sure."

"This place is amazing," she exclaimed, and Georgiana was glad that her mother was undoubtedly so taken with the surroundings that she hadn't noticed the exchange between either Landon and Pete...or Landon and Georgiana.

"Mrs. Camp always picks the nicest places for her recitals," Eden continued.

Georgiana nodded. "Yes, she does." Mrs. Camp did attempt to make the children feel extra special on recital day, and she had definitely managed that feat with Abi. Georgiana's little girl hadn't stopped talking about how she and her friends would play their music on a stage with paintings all around them. *"Even the painters will be there listening to us!"* Abi had said.

Mrs. Camp got the whole town keyed up about the children's big day. From what Eden had told Georgiana, Gina Brown had advertised the event for weeks and was even hosting a wet-paint sale from several local artists after the recital. And Mrs. Camp had arranged for the Sweet Spot to provide desserts and for Claremont's new coffee shop The Grind to serve specialty coffees and teas.

"Georgiana, the gallery is like a renovated warehouse, with high ceilings and exposed pipes," Eden said. "And there are local painters sporadically all around, some painting landscapes and others painting flowers. One is working on a horse painting."

"Hey, maybe you could get some of Gina Brown's artwork to hang in the fishing cabins, make them look cozy," Georgiana said.

"You know what, that's a great idea. I'll talk to her about that. We only need one now, since we've only got the blue cabin done, so maybe I can get something from the wet-paint sale."

"When is the banker coming out to see the place?" Eden asked.

"John is going to meet with Andy Tuesday after he finishes his classes at Stockville to present the business plan. They'll set up the appointment for Andy to come out and see the finished cabin."

"It's a great idea," Eden said.

"Yeah, I think it is too," Landon agreed, then squeezed Georgiana's hand. "We've named that first cabin 'Georgiana's Place' after the person who had the idea."

That was the first Georgiana had heard of the cabins being named. "Really?"

"It's already painted above the door."

She leaned over and kissed him on the cheek. "Thanks."

"You're welcome."

"Oh," Eden said softly.

"What is it, Mom?"

"Just, well, if looks could kill, Landon would be a dead man right now."

"He had his chance," Landon said.

Georgiana didn't know what Pete was doing or how he looked at Landon now, but she didn't have time to ask. Mrs. Camp's voice filled the air as she announced the first young pianist.

Probably because she was the newest student, Abi was the last to perform. Mrs. Camp announced her, and then Georgiana heard her footsteps cross the stage.

"Come on, sweetie," she whispered. Then she heard the piano bench scoot against the floor, and then the first notes filled the air as Abi played the simple piece. Georgiana had listened to Abi practice it repeatedly over the past few weeks, but knowing that a large portion of Claremont now filled the gallery and was completely silent to listen to her little girl play—and knowing that she'd garnered the courage to be here too—made Georgiana's eyes fill. The tears spilled over and continued until she, and the remainder of the room, applauded Abi's precious performance.

"She did amazing," Landon said, then placed a handkerchief in Georgiana's hand. "I had a feeling you might need this tonight."

She dabbed at her eyes. "You were right."

Abi darted to them as soon as Mrs. Camp announced the program had completed. "How'd you like it?"

"You were wonderful," Georgiana said, accepting Abi's hug and kissing the top of her daughter's soft curls. "Incredible."

"You were amazing, Abi!" Pete said.

"Thanks, Daddy! I've been practicing real hard."

"I could tell."

Georgiana felt odd listening to him so easily step into Abi's world, but this was something that she would have to deal with from now on. Might as well get used to it. At least he lived in Tampa, so she didn't have to deal with him on a daily basis.

"Listen, I didn't think about asking you to bring a change of clothes tonight, but I was wondering if you'd like to stay with us over at Aunt Jan's house tonight? It's your cousin Lance's birthday, and they're having his party tonight. I thought you'd like to go and see everyone. We could go get your things at the farm in a little while."

"Is that okay, Mommy?" Abi asked.

Georgiana couldn't say no to Abi spending time at Pete's sister's home. "Yes, that's fine."

"Oh, but Grandma and I were gonna celebrate my first recital with a double chocolate milk shake."

"We can celebrate another day," Eden said. "I won't forget. I think I like Nelson's milk shakes even more than you do. You go have fun at Lance's party. And I think I'm going to look at all of these pretty paintings they have for sale and maybe buy one for your room."

"I'd like a horse one or a rabbit one," Abi said.

"Then that's what I'll look for."

"You ready, Daddy?"

"I sure am."

Abi gave Georgiana another hug. "Thank you for coming, Mommy, and for wearing your new dress. I told you it'd be fun tonight. It was, wasn't it?"

"Yes, sweetie, it was."

"I love you, Momma," Abi said, squeezing Georgiana even harder, and Georgiana heard Pete's low groan.

"Come on, Abi. The party has probably already started."

Georgiana listened to their footsteps fade.

"You okay?" Landon slid his hand against hers and twined their fingers.

"Yes, I'm okay. At least he wasn't too mean."

"I wouldn't say he was nice," Eden said, "but I guess he wasn't overly mean either."

Landon squeezed her hand. "The important thing is that Abi did great and was extra happy because you came to see her perform." He touched the satin strap of her red dress. "And you wore your new red dress."

Georgiana lifted a foot. "And cute shoes."

"Very cute shoes," he agreed.

"I'm proud of you, honey." Eden kissed her cheek. "Now, are you two staying around a while or heading on back to the farm?"

"I think we should probably leave so I can get Abi's things together before Pete comes over."

"Good idea," Eden said. "I'm going to see about getting a painting for Abi's room. Do you want me to look for something for one of the fishing cabins too?"

"That'd be great," Landon said. "Something outdoorsy. A landscape scene or horses."

"Or a rabbit," Georgiana said, smiling. "It is 'Georgiana's Place,' after all."

He laughed. "Or a rabbit."

They left the gallery and started back to the farm, while Georgiana pondered how to tell Landon everything that was on her heart. She'd made it through her first big public outing and being around Pete again with hardly any discomfort because she'd been by Landon's side. Being with him felt right, and she never wanted to be anywhere else.

So she had to tell him two things.

One, that she loved him, with all her heart. And two, that she hadn't been completely honest about what caused her blindness. The first would undoubtedly make him happy. But the second…

"You're mighty quiet," he said, turning off the engine as they apparently arrived at the farm. She'd had no idea they'd already driven that far. "What's on your mind, Georgie?"

She took a deep breath. "You. Us." Then she shivered, and she wasn't certain if it was because of the chill in the air or because of her fear. *Please God, let him understand why I haven't told him before now.*

"You're cold," he said. "Let's go inside and get warm, and then we can talk about what's on your mind." He paused. "Because I'm pretty sure the same thing is on my mind." His door slammed as he exited the car.

Her heart thumped solidly in her chest. He loved her; she was certain of it. If only she could simply tell him she loved him too and let that be it, then live happily ever after. She really wanted a happily ever after with Landon.

He opened her door and helped her out, then they went into the house. "You want to get Abi's things together first, in case they show up soon?"

"I probably should." Georgiana had almost forgotten about getting Abi clothes for spending the night at her aunt's house. She went upstairs to Abi's room, found the small suitcase under her bed and began filling it with everything she'd need for an overnight stay. She knew her daughter's clothes as well as her own, so she easily packed the bag. But just as she started back down the stairs, a loud knock sounded at the front door.

"I've got it." Landon's footsteps echoed across

the floor and then she heard him open the door just as she reached the bottom step.

"Pete, Georgiana's getting Abi's things," Landon said, civil but definitely not friendly.

"I see her. She's right behind you," Pete's words were delivered with so much hate Georgiana could feel the anger. "Can't you see her, or are you blind too?"

"You wanting trouble, Pete?"

"Landon, Pete!" Georgiana said, taking the few steps between the bottom of the stairs and the door. She stepped into Landon, then moved aside and held out the bag. "Here, take her bag, Pete. And leave, please."

"What are you doing, Georgiana? And what are you doing, Cutter? What, do you feel guilty about what you did? Is that why you're with her? Because it seems like you'd have come back years ago, after the damage was done. Our marriage would have been fine if it wasn't for you."

"What are you talking about?" Landon asked, while Georgiana's head throbbed. This couldn't be happening. Not tonight, not when she'd planned to tell him.

"Pete, no," she begged.

But Pete wasn't having any part of her request. "Of course it took her years before she told me. But you—you knew—and you stayed gone. Now you come back? You leave her blind and expect me to take care of the damaged goods, and when I don't, then you're going to pick up the pieces? Georgiana, is that what you want, someone who's with you out of pity?"

"Pete, I mean it, if you don't tell me what you're talking about, right now..." Landon warned.

Then the pieces seemed to click into place for Pete; Georgiana heard his gasp when he put it all together. And laughed. An evil, sinister laugh.

"Georgiana, is there something you need to tell your boyfriend?"

"Pete, don't do this. I was going to tell him tonight, and there's no reason to hurt me this way."

"Tell me what, Georgie?"

"No reason to hurt you? I'm not the one who hurt you, Georgiana, he is. And it's about time somebody told him." He cleared his throat, while Georgiana's tears burned free. "You see, Landon, after several years of marriage and no telling how many marriage-counseling sessions, she finally decided to open up and tell me the truth about what happened in the church that day."

Georgiana could only imagine Landon's face, but Pete must have seen what she imagined.

"That's right. She told me about your profession of love two days before our wedding. And then she told me about how she was running away from you, how she ran out of that church because she'd gotten so upset at what you'd said and she pulled out in front of that truck."

"That's not what I said," Georgiana interjected. Pete was changing the story, and if he continued, then Landon would be even more hurt. "I told you that I left the church because—"

"Let him finish, Georgie." Landon's words were strained, and hurt. She'd waited too long to tell him the truth, and she'd opened the door for Pete to hurt him even more.

"But what you don't realize is that her injuries from that wreck weren't resolved during that first hospital stay. See that wreck—the wreck you caused—came back to haunt us just a few months later, when she started losing her vision. And then, well, you know what happened next. I had a blind wife, thanks to you."

"Georgie, is that true?" Landon asked, and she really didn't want to answer. "Is it?"

"Tell him, Georgiana. It isn't like I made that up."

"I wasn't running from you," she said. "I left that church because I realized that I had feelings for you."

"Which means that marrying me made all the sense in the world," Pete spouted. "I'm out of here. Our daughter is waiting at Jan's house." His steps were hard against the porch as he stomped his way to his car.

"Landon, I was going to tell you tonight."

"You said they weren't sure what caused your blindness. I asked you, and you said the doctors weren't sure."

"They weren't sure what happened in the wreck that actually caused it," she stammered.

"Georgie, you knew it was the wreck. You knew that I caused it, and yet you never told me. You didn't get word to me what had happened when I left in the army, and you never told me the truth now. I thought—I really thought you trusted me."

"I wanted to tell you tonight. I was going to. I wanted to tell you that I love you, and I knew I couldn't tell you that unless there were no secrets between us. So I was going to tell you."

"Why should I believe you now?" he asked, and, heaven help her, she didn't have an answer.

"Landon," she started, but he'd already turned away, his footsteps slow and determined as he left her house and broke her heart.

Chapter Fifteen

Landon drove all over Claremont and then to Stockville while he thought about everything Pete had said. And the whole time he kept replaying that day at the church, his confession of love for Georgie, her running away and then the sound of her car getting hit by that truck.

His mind jumped to the hospital, seeing her in the hospital bed black-and-blue from the wreck, and then telling her how sorry he was. She'd told him she couldn't see him anymore and that she was still marrying Pete.

And then he'd left Claremont.

And she'd gone blind.

He slammed his fist against the steering wheel. Why hadn't he checked on her again? Why hadn't she told him when she realized what had happened?

Because she'd married Pete, his mind whispered, *and Georgiana marries for life.*

His conversation with her on the ridge came back to him with utter clarity.

"I had to drive, had to think. I thought I would ride around town for a while and then find Mom, talk to her and see what she thought about what I believed I simply had to do."

"What you had to do?"

"Cancel the wedding."

Landon had no doubt she'd told him the truth that day. And then again tonight. She did leave that church because of him, but it wasn't like Pete said. She wasn't trying to get away from Landon. She was running to him.

And yes, she was wrong in keeping the blindness from him. She was wrong in not telling him that the wreck caused the blindness. But she was only trying to honor the marriage vow she'd taken with Pete. And she said she was going to tell Landon about it all tonight, and right now, he realized...he believed her.

He turned the truck around. Back then, at that church, she'd been running to him. Now it was time for him to run to her.

His cell phone rang as he headed back toward Claremont. He glanced at the display and answered. "Eden, I'm on my way back. Let her know. I'm sorry she's upset."

"Georgiana isn't with you? She isn't answering her cell."

"She isn't with me. Did you call the house?"

"I did, and she didn't answer. I'm still at the square. You said she was upset?"

"Yeah, she was, but I'm on my way back."

"I'll start home. Why was she upset, Landon? What did Pete do?"

"It was me this time," he said, disconnecting and then pressing the pedal to the floor.

God, please, let her be okay.

Landon arrived at her farm and noticed Eden hadn't made it home. He pulled beside the porch, slammed his foot on the brake, turned off the truck and jumped out. "Georgiana!" He jumped up the steps, opened the door to the house and yelled her name again.

No response.

Where would she have gone? His eyes moved to the barn. Fallon. "Georgie!" he yelled again.

A strangled sound echoed from the barn, and Landon jumped off the porch and took off running. He rounded the corner to the barn so quickly that his boots slid on the hay, and he grabbed the edge to keep from falling, peered inside...and saw her.

Another piercing sob rang out as she struggled to put the saddle on her horse. Her cries were escaping so forcefully that she apparently hadn't heard him yell her name.

"Georgiana!" he yelled again, and this time, she stopped, turned and let the saddle drop to the ground.

"Landon?" She sucked in air, grabbed her chest. "Landon, I was trying to find you! I'm so sorry I didn't tell you. I had to find you and let you know…I love—" She never got a chance to finish. He closed the distance between them, took her in his arms and kissed her forehead, her cheeks, her lips. He couldn't stop kissing her, holding her, loving her.

"*I'm* sorry, Georgie. You were going to tell me tonight. I believe you. And you didn't tell me before because you'd been committed to Pete. I'm sure it was tough for me to come back after all this time and then you instantly open up to me, especially after what you went through with Pete. I should have understood, but I didn't, and I left you…again." He kissed her once more. "But I won't leave you, if you'll let me stay. I love you, Georgie. I've loved you for as long as I can remember. And I don't want to be away from you again."

She wrapped her arms around him. "Oh, Landon, I do love you, with all my heart I do."

"Well, it looks like I don't need to look for her

anymore?" Eden's voice echoed through the barn. "Georgiana, don't ever scare us like that again."

"I won't," she said, smiling against Landon's chest. "I don't have any reason to run away anymore."

"Actually, you weren't running away," Landon reminded. "You were running *to*."

She smiled again. "You're right, I was."

Epilogue

❧

"I got a little wedding present for the groom."
Andy Cothran entered the front room of the
Claremont Community Church where Landon,
John and Casey waited to be cued. He waved a
folded paper in his hand.

Landon winked at John. "Wonder what that is."

"What is it?" Casey asked. He'd come home for
the wedding, and his brothers still hadn't let him
in on their upcoming business venture. They'd
wanted to make sure the bank was on board first,
and it appeared they were getting their wish.

"What is this?" Andy echoed. "Why, it's one
of the most innovative business plans I've seen in
quite a while." He handed the paper to Landon.
"And it's been approved. Y'all have six months to
get your fishing camp up and running, and I've got
a feeling you're gonna make it happen. We really
liked what we saw with that first finished cabin.

Thinking I might actually take my granddaughter out there once you get the place rolling."

"That'd be great," Landon said, tucking the paper into his pocket.

"And congratulations. You've got a great girl there you're marrying."

"I'd have to agree." Landon grinned at the man as he left the room.

"We're starting a fishing camp?" Casey asked. "I leave for college, and Landon decides to get married, and y'all decide to start a fishing camp. Anything else I need to know?"

"Yeah, the next business will be a dude ranch, but we haven't finalized that business plan yet," John said.

Landon shook his head. "I didn't hear Andy say anything about a dude ranch."

"That's because it's gonna be the *next* business plan. I'll keep you posted. You just worry about getting this wedding done right."

Landon laughed. "You do that, and I will."

"Y'all never got involved in all this kind of stuff when I was at home," Casey said.

"Yeah, we had to wait till you left to have some real fun," John said, and Landon laughed again. He loved having his brothers together, and he loved all of them being happy again.

The door opened, and Brother Henry nodded at the trio. "It's time, boys."

Boys. Landon guessed they'd always be boys to their preacher. So they didn't argue, and the *boys* walked out to find nearly all of Claremont waiting in the church pews on the other side.

"Is Georgiana ready for this?" John whispered.

"We're about to find out."

Landon smiled as Abi, wearing a gold dress and with her hair in adorable ringlets, stepped down the aisle smiling and waving as she tossed rose petals and created a colorful yellow-and-burgundy path for his bride.

Mandy Brantley came next. She'd been a true friend to Georgie back in high school and the two had grown close ever since that night at the square, particularly in the past few weeks when Georgiana planned the wedding. People didn't typically get married in October, but neither Landon nor Georgiana wanted to wait any longer. Mandy had been a pro at getting everything lined up and in order.

The music ended, and the first bars of the "Bridal Chorus" played while Landon watched and waited for his bride. He'd been waiting for her his entire life, and finally, within a matter of minutes, she'd be his.

He'd never wanted anything more.

The entire room stood to see Eden walking Georgiana down the aisle.

Her dress was a combination of satin and lace, fitted at the top and flowing at the bottom. But it wasn't the dress that Landon noticed the most. Her hair was long and flowing in soft strawberry curls, exactly the way he liked it. But that wasn't what he noticed the most. Her face was flawless, not overly done with makeup, and he was happy to see the sprinkle of copper freckles across her nose and cheeks as she neared him at the front of the church.

But that wasn't what he noticed the most.

What held his attention, what touched his soul, was her eyes. The hazel shone vibrantly today as she seemed to search him out with every step. The gold flakes catching the light and making them shine. And even though he knew she couldn't see him with those beautiful eyes, Landon knew she did see him now…with her heart.

Brother Henry recited the ceremony, and Landon's heart pounded so loudly he had to focus to hear each word. Because he wanted to hear everything. He wanted to remember everything. This was the beginning of the rest of their lives.

"Landon," Brother Henry repeated.

He looked at her eyes, her smile. "I love you," he said, and several in the audience laughed softly.

"He said you can kiss Mommy," Abi announced, which caused several more laughs.

Georgie whispered, "Landon, one time you told me you wanted to be the one to kiss me in this church." She smiled. "Now's your chance."

And, amid the sounds of cheers, applause and Abi's giggles, he did.

* * * * *

Be sure to look for Renee Andrews's
next Love Inspired novel,
HEART OF A RANCHER,
coming in March 2013!

Dear Reader,

Some of life's most crucial decisions are made in those late teenage years, when hormones are still out of whack and emotions are running wild. It always amazes me when, later on in life, I run into someone from my teens who says, "I never told you, but…" You can fill in the blank.

I'm hoping *Love Reunited* will open your mind and heart to the possibility of addressing a situation rather than ignoring it. But, as we learned in the book, everything happens for a reason. And God has a plan. I love that His plan for this book had Landon, Georgiana and Abi all together in the end!

I enjoy mixing facts and fiction in my novels, and you'll learn about some of the truths hidden within the story on my website, www.reneeandrews.com. You can even see the actual tattoo from Landon's wrist, because it is an actual tattoo on the inner wrist of Chief Warrant Officer 2 Johnny Matherne, Jr. That tattoo gave me inspiration for creating Landon Cutter's character. While you're at my site, you can also enter contests for cool prizes.

Blessings in Christ,
Renee Andrews

Questions for Discussion

1. Both Georgiana and Landon were devastated when their close friendship ended. Have you ever been in a similar situation? Please discuss.

2. How hard is it to rekindle a warm friendship that has grown cold, either by circumstance or by neglect?

3. So many teens find it difficult to share their feelings the way Georgiana and Landon found it difficult. Does this also happen with adults? What can we do to overcome this fear?

4. Georgiana's husband, Pete, couldn't handle it when Georgie lost her sight. Why do you think this is? How could he have done things differently?

5. Landon and Pete could not be more different. Are there qualities that one has that the other doesn't?

6. Landon mentions that many people aren't sure how to react or what to say when they meet someone who has fought for their country in the military. Do you find it easy to talk

to and appreciate those who have served in the armed forces?

7. John doesn't enjoy working at the steel plant, but he does it without complaint because it is necessary. Do you know people who sacrifice for their family this way? Are you making sacrifices for your family? Discuss.

8. John helps Casey go to college. Landon helps John. When times are tough, their family pulls together. On the other hand, when times are tough for Pete, he pulls away. What makes people either grow closer or apart during tough times?

9. Georgiana thinks her wreck is God's way of telling her to stay with Pete. Do you ever find yourself trying to determine what God meant or didn't mean by an action?

10. Georgiana is afraid to go into town on her own and tries her best to avoid it when possible. Have you ever found yourself going out of your way to avoid a task? Why or why not?

11. Landon offers to help Georgiana learn how to ride a horse. Is this a selfless offer on Landon's part, or does he have ulterior motives?

12. Aside from her blindness, Georgiana has a young daughter. Does her single-motherhood ever deter Landon from pursuing a relationship with Georgiana? Have you ever known other men who were unsure about dating a single mom?

Love Inspired® SUSPENSE

RIVETING INSPIRATIONAL ROMANCE

Watch for our series of edge-
of-your-seat suspense novels.
These contemporary tales
of intrigue and romance
feature Christian characters
facing challenges to their faith...
and their lives!

AVAILABLE IN REGULAR
& LARGER-PRINT FORMATS

For exciting stories that reflect traditional values,
visit:
www.ReaderService.com